Wrong City

A NOVEL

Morgan Richter

Luft
Books

Copyright © 2010-2013 Morgan Richter

Published in the United States by Luft Books, New York.
www.luftbooks.com

First paperback edition December 2013

IBSN 978-0-9859768-7-3

Cover design by Morgan Dodge

To Ingrid.

CHAPTER ONE

THE PARTY WAS already on the decline when the girl in the bumblebee dress climbed onto the patio railing. Silhouetted by the Los Angeles skyline, which crawled along the horizon in an unbroken stretch of glittery lights, she stood on the slim beam and wobbled.

Vish watched her, his hands clutching his near-depleted bamboo tray of bite-sized chimichangas. She shouldn't be doing that. One wrong step, one wobble too far, and this girl, whoever she was, would tumble into the darkness of the canyon below, gone forever. Vish couldn't see anything beyond the reach of the lamps at the edge of the patio; where their light ended, blackness began and swept down the hillside, stopped only by the barricade of sparkly lights that marked Hollywood Boulevard.

There were murmurs from the guests: amusement, disapproval, no overt concern. The girl shifted sideways, one tiny foot in front of the other on the railing, arms raised at her sides, poised like a gymnast preparing to execute a flip.

Not that a gymnast would wear those shoes. They were shiny leather—the stark light from the lamps drained color from everything it touched, so Vish couldn't be sure, but he thought they were bright blue—with pointy toes and skinny gold spikes for heels. She wasn't really dressed as a bumble-

1

bee, not literally, but that'd been Vish's immediate thought upon seeing her. Her dress was short and strapless, made from a narrow length of ruffled yellow taffeta wrapped around and around her tiny body until her waist looked wider than her slight shoulders. A black fringe dangled from the ruffle, giving the impression of horizontal stripes that shifted and rippled as she moved. It was belted with a wide black satin sash, the ends of which spilled down to her ankles. She could trip on them, lose her balance, fall to her death.

Someone should stop her. He should stop her. Vish hovered near the patio door.

"Better watch your step, Kels," a woman called out from the crowd. She laughed, teeth glinting in the patio lights. Her face glistened with perspiration, and to Vish's eyes she looked slithery and unearthly, a golem calling for the blood of this girl.

The girl—Kels?—shook her head. She had a mess of pale hair, cut short and jagged, which stuck up like a cloud of downy fluff around her head. She was very pretty, in a child-like way, and she seemed much too young to be at this party, amongst this collection of directors and producers and sundry members of the entertainment industry. The bulk of the guests were in their forties or beyond, Vish guessed, though it was hard to be certain with all the lean, toned bodies and tight, unlined skin on display.

"I'm fine," the girl said. Her voice was light and babyish. "Look, I'm perfectly balanced." She pivoted on the railing, pointed toes shifting smartly, until she faced the guests. "I could do a cartwheel on here."

2

She seemed sober, at least. Clear eyes, no flushed skin, no slurred speech. Still, Vish felt his stomach clench in anticipation of something terrible. Should he step in and haul her down from there? Should he find the hostess and alert her to the possible tragedy and/or lawsuit waiting to happen on her patio?

The girl glanced over her pale shoulder. "I can't even see the bottom," she said. "If I fell, they'd have to wait until morning to look for me."

A man angled through the assembled guests and approached the railing. Laughing, he held a hand up to her. "Time to come down, darling," he said.

The girl smiled. She had a dimple in each cheek. She crouched and took his hand in her own dainty one, then hopped down to the patio floor. She wobbled on the gold spikes when she landed, but she stayed upright.

Vish's stomach relaxed. His face felt hot. Silly to get so worked up; she was fine. She'd been fine all along, she was having a good time, and he was an overprotective ninny. It was just the combination of the crowd, and the looming blackness beyond the patio, and maybe something in the night air that made him feel anxious.

The girl tilted her face up and pecked the man on his jaw. "You always take such good care of me," she said.

Huh. The man was probably in his early thirties, a few years older than Vish, and thus was too old to be her date. He was pretty, slim and foxlike, with glossy black hair worn long in front, short in back. Dark eyes, a mad fringe of black eyelashes, dark golden skin.

The man murmured something to the girl that Vish couldn't hear. She giggled in reply, then released him and drifted off into the crowd.

So they weren't a couple, or probably weren't. Vish looked at the man, aware of the combination of gratitude and envy he felt for the easy way he took charge of the situation. He wore what was almost certainly a terribly expensive suit, with sleek lines and a burnished shimmer to the fabric. He didn't look familiar exactly, but he looked like someone Vish should know, like his life would be richer and more interesting for including him in his circle of acquaintances.

He was here to work, not to ogle the guests. His sad little tray of chimichangas was cold. He entered through the open French doors into the heart of the party.

He skidded on the floor, which was made of raised, rounded tiles, polished until they gleamed. In his best shoes, Vish could barely walk without wobbling or sliding. From behind him, a hand clamped around his upper arm, holding him in place.

He glanced back at his assailant, a fierce, compact woman in a sleeveless batik-patterned dress that displayed her ropy biceps to full effect. It was the hostess, Maryanne something-or-other, and she looked furious. Her grip on Vish's arm tightened; her thin lips twisted into a snarl.

She didn't look at him. Her attention was fixed on the far end of the living room where Jamie, her own empty tray held by her side, was cornered by a middle-aged man with a tidy beard.

Ah. Maryanne's husband. Jamie had pointed him out to Vish and Toby while they were loading their trays in the kitchen earlier.

"She's supposed to be serving guests, not schmoozing," Maryanne said. Her forehead creased, her sculpted eyebrows almost touching. "It's unprofessional."

If Jamie was schmoozing, she was doing a poor job of it. The man carried on what appeared to be a lively monologue while Jamie nodded at frequent intervals, her blonde ponytail bobbing up and down. Her expression showed nothing but polite interest, but she seemed to be recoiling from him, pressing herself against the sofa in the hopes it would swallow her up.

"Every time I've looked at her, she's been gabbing with my husband. This isn't a networking event for the caterers. She's not going to get cast in one of his films just because she served him a taco."

Vish cleared his throat. "You know, I really don't think she's trying—"

"I don't want to get her in trouble, but I'm a step away from going into the kitchen and telling her boss."

Vish paused. The only one in the kitchen was Toby, and the idea of Toby as anyone's boss seemed ludicrous. "Ah... she's in charge. She owns the company."

Maryanne looked at him for the first time. The forehead crease deepened. Vish hastened to continue. "I'll pass your concerns along to her."

"Do that." Maryanne shifted her attention back to Jamie. "She's an actress, isn't she?"

"She does this full-time now."

"But she used to act, didn't she? She's got that actressy look." The snarl relaxed into a contemptuous smirk. "It's a cliché because it's true: Everyone in the service industry in this town is a wannabe movie star."

Vish smiled. "I'm not," he said.

Maryanne glanced at him again. Her expression shifted again. She looked puzzled. "No, of course you're not," she said. Like she was explaining something obvious to someone who had difficulty with simple concepts.

Vish took a moment to sort that one out. Maryanne pointed her chin at Jamie. "Talk to her. I spend a lot of money on my parties, and my friends value my recommendations. Right now, I don't think I have much good to say about you people."

Vish nodded. "Sure. Of course. No problem."

Maryanne looked unappeased. She maintained her death-grip on his arm. It hurt. At a loss for a graceful way to free himself, he proffered his tray. "Chimichanga?"

Success. She released him. One hand hovered above the tray, then she hesitated. "Those are eggrolls?" she asked.

"Chimichangas. Like little deep-fried burritos," Vish said.

She grimaced and shook her head. "I don't eat anything fried." The hand withdrew. She stalked off, expertly navigating the rounded tiles in her spike-heeled sandals.

At a low chuckle behind him, Vish turned. Ah. The pretty man from the patio. "No, of course you're not an actor," the man said in a perfect imitation of Maryanne. "Whatever do you suppose she meant by that?"

Vish smiled. "I'm sure it wasn't flattering," he said. "I imagine she was saying I'm insufficiently cute to be a movie star."

"Says her," the man said. He winked. "Could be simple bias, you know. She could be saying you're insufficiently white to be a movie star."

His tone was casual, almost flippant. The man was nearly as dark as Vish, though it was tough to pinpoint his ethnic background. Latino? Filipino? Neither seemed quite right.

No way was Vish was going to be lured into chatting about the party's hostess while standing in the middle of her living room, surrounded by her guests. He held up his tray. "Chimichanga?"

The man glanced at the offering on display. "God, no," he said. He waggled his empty glass. "Can you get me a refill, or do I fetch it myself?"

Jamie didn't have a liquor license. Maryanne had hired the bartender separately, and the libations didn't fall into Vish's territory. He took the glass from the man. "I can get it. What are you having?"

"Scotch. Dude at the bar will know what. Thanks."

The bar was set up in the sunken dining room, through a narrow archway bordered with hand-painted ceramic tiles. "I need a Scotch," Vish said to the bartender, a sullen kid with hair winched back into a low ponytail.

The kid looked skeptical. Vish shook his head. "Not for me. For that guy," he said. He pointed through the arch in the direction of the pretty man. "He said you'd know what he was drinking."

The bartender scowled. "Him. Yeah." He fingered his way through a selection of bottles atop the rolling cart that served as a portable bar, picked one, and tossed a few cubes into a fresh glass. "Rocks, water, right?"

"I have no idea."

The bartender shrugged, fixed the drink, and handed over the glass. "Here you go."

"Thanks. Do you know who he is? That man?"

"Never seen him before, but everyone here is acting like he's the shit. Probably a studio exec or whatever. He's got a stupid name, Stubby or Stumpy or something."

The pretty man didn't look like a Stubby, or a Stumpy. Vish glanced at him again. He was now at the center of a small throng, deep in conversation with a cluster of party guests, the girl in the bumblebee dress among them. She snaked her arm up his back and hooked her hand over his shoulder, her body curving into his. He seemed unaware of her presence, his attention fixed on the bearded host. Good to see Jamie had finally escaped his clutches.

"Open calls only sound like a good idea, but they're more hassle than they're worth," the host was saying. "I found this great kid last month—good-looking guy, theater background, an absolute nobody but perfect for the part, so I took a gamble and cast him. A week into shooting, he disappears on me. Doesn't show up at his call time, doesn't answer his phone. I sent a PA over to his apartment to pound on his door, but no dice. We're going to have to recast ASAP."

"Rough break," the pretty man said.

"You're telling me. Now there's a whole list of re-shoots I've got to get through, all because the kid turned out to be a goddamned flake." He chuckled. "Of course, if it turns out he died or something, I'm going to sound like a real douche here, right?"

The pretty man nodded. "Been hearing a lot of that these days. I mean actors disappearing, not you sounding like a douche. Seems to be an epidemic." He reached out and accepted his drink from Vish. "Thanks, man," he said. A smile and another wink. Friendly. Flirtatious, maybe. Hard to tell.

Vish smiled back and withdrew.

The chimichangas looked sadder than ever. He headed into the kitchen, which was connected through another archway, one step down from the dining room, which itself was a step down from the living room. Between the slick tiles and the steps in unexpected places, someone was going to trip over his feet and break his neck before the end of the night. That someone would probably be Vish.

In the kitchen, Jamie reloaded her tray with hot hors d'oeuvres. She dumped a handful of crumbled Manchego over pumpkin empanadas, their flaky crusts brown from the oven. "There. That should prevent confusion, right?" she asked. "I've had two guests complain that they thought these would be sweet, like miniature pumpkin pies. The pork in the filling really threw them off." She glanced up at Vish. "Everything going okay out there?"

"Fine," he said. He paused. "Maryanne saw you talking to her husband." He made it as light as possible.

Jamie looked at him. Her expression sharpened. She nodded once. "Ah," she said. "How are the chimichangas going over?"

"Hard to say," he said. "Eggrolls are fried, right?"

"Of course. Why?"

Vish shrugged. "Just asking."

Toby hauled a hot cookie sheet out of the oven and plunked it down on the tile counter. Jamie hurried to maneuver a potholder beneath it. The sheet held an array of miniature chicken tacos, the corn tortillas translucent with hot grease. "Hey, did you see Kelsey?" Toby asked.

"Who?"

Both Toby and Jamie turned to stare at him. "Kelsey Kirkpatrick," Jamie said, the incredulity plain in her voice. "From *Interstellar Boys*?"

Vish shook his head. "I don't have a television right now," he said. From billboards and bus advertisements, he was aware of the existence of a series named *Interstellar Boys*, but he wasn't familiar enough with it to recognize the cast members.

"She's the hot little blonde thing. Come on. You've seen her," Toby said.

"The girl in the bumblebee dress?"

Jamie giggled. "Bumblebee dress," she said. "For gosh sakes, Vish, that's a Frederic Lanchin. It's couture." Jamie's Texas roots sometimes came out in unguarded moments, and she pronounced it "couchure."

"She's hot," Toby said.

"She is?" Vish spread a clean black cloth napkin on his tray and began arranging the tacos in what he hoped was an aesthetically pleasing display. "She seemed so young." He pictured the girl teetering on the railing, her round face and downy-chick hairstyle and baby-doll voice. The idea of her as an object of anyone's fierce passion seemed absurd, like lusting after a stuffed animal.

"Eighteen in six weeks, man. Six weeks. Can't wait."

"For what? So you can drool over her?" Jamie opened the oven door a crack, peeked in on whatever was still in there, closed it. "Kinda seems like you're doing plenty of that already, sugar."

"So I can drool after her legally. Without feeling creepy about it." Toby shrugged. "Biological imperative, babe."

Vish wasn't sure what that meant, and he wasn't sure the sentiment bore careful parsing, either. Freshly-loaded tray in hand, he glanced through the archway into the dining room. The pretty man was in his line of sight, deep in conversation with Maryanne and her husband. "Hey, do either of you know that guy talking to the hosts?"

Jamie glanced over and shrugged. "No idea. Why?"

"Not sure. He looks familiar, sort of. Like he's someone I'm supposed to know."

"He's foxy," Jamie said. She nudged her elbow into his ribs and winked. "Are you interested?"

"That's not why I was asking."

"No offense meant. Just checking. You keep to yourself so much it's hard to know where your interests lie."

Toby squinted at the man. "I think he's just some guy," he said at last.

That seemed to be the final word on the matter, so Vish headed out into the party once more.

CHAPTER TWO

THE PARTY DEFLATED shortly thereafter. Guests seeped out and slipped off into the night; the noise level ebbed. It was still before midnight when Jamie, Toby and Vish began loading foil-wrapped trays of leftovers into the stubby white company van.

The night air was a relief after the stuffy kitchen. Vish could smell hot grease and smoke clinging to his hair and clothes. The back of the van reeked of chorizo and corn oil.

Toby scrambled into the passenger seat. That meant Vish would be nestled in back with the leftovers. His stomach lurched.

"You won't need me to unload, will you?" he asked. "I'm opening the shop in the morning. Would you mind if I just took off from here?"

Jamie looked at him, confused. "You mean walk?"

"Just down the hill. I can catch a bus when I hit Hollywood."

"It's fine with me, but it's an awful long way to the beach. Let me drop you off at the shop. That'll get you a whole lot closer to your place."

"No, I'm fine. I could use some air," Vish said. "Is there anything I should know for tomorrow?"

Jamie thought for a moment. "Should be pretty straight-forward. Someone's coming in for a tasting in the morning, but I left everything marked in the fridge. That's about it." She paused. "Are you absolutely sure I can't give you a ride? It's late. It might be dangerous."

"I'm sure. Exercise will do me some good." Jamie was right. It was a long way to Venice Beach, and the buses at night were infrequent and erratic, but the urge for solitude trumped that right now. "I'll see you on Monday, okay?"

"Sure thing, sugar. Thanks for all your help tonight." Jamie looked concerned, but not like she was going to push the issue. With a wave, she climbed up into the front seat.

Jamie and Toby drove off down the canyon road. Vish followed on foot. No sidewalk, so he kept to the gravel shoulder. The road was narrow and twisty and dark, the only illumination provided by the glow of the city below. A moonless night, the sky inky and impenetrable.

All was quiet. Rare to find this kind of tranquil darkness in the middle of Los Angeles. The air smelled good, like eucalyptus and lemon verbena and damp earth. Early September, and the air was crisp, but not chilly.

He heard a rustle in the shrubbery forming a loose barrier between the road and the steep slope of the canyon, a crunching of pebbles, a stirring of dead leaves. A coyote, maybe, one of the many that roamed the hills in packs, sometimes wandering into town and dragging off the occasional family pet. They avoided humans, Vish had heard, but all the same, he quickened his pace a little.

He was crossing beside a parked car, something sleek and sumptuous, when he heard a voice: "Hey."

He turned. Leaning against the hood, arms folded across his chest, was the pretty man. Vish could barely see him in the darkness. "You didn't park on the hill?" the man asked.

"Hey. No, I'm catching the bus," Vish said. He paused. "Car trouble?"

The man shrugged. "Can't get it to start."

"What's wrong with it?" Vish asked. Not that he'd have any idea how to fix it, but it seemed only polite to ask.

Another shrug. "Not sure. I'm not really a car person, you know? Never had the interest." He straightened up, popped the hood. Gestured for Vish to look closer. "At a guess, though, I'd say this might be the problem."

A chaos of smashed parts. It looked like someone had wielded a sledgehammer and bashed everything, all that finely-tuned German engineering, into crushed bits. "Wow," Vish said. He looked at the man. "Who did that?"

"Don't know." He smiled. Very white teeth, shining in the darkness. His incisors were too long, giving him the impression of fangs. "I probably deserved it, though."

He said it in such a matter-of-fact way that Vish wasn't sure he was joking. There was something frightening about this level of destruction, that someone had directed so much rage and fury toward him in this specific manner. Cars were an extension of everyone's personalities here in Los Angeles. In the eyes of many, Vish's lack of his own car marked him as somehow incomplete, less than a wholly functioning human being. The attack on the car was an attack on the man.

Vish glanced around. The rustling in the bushes, the dark night, the empty road… "Do you want me to call you a cab?"

"A friend's picking me up. Thanks, though." The man looked thoughtful, but not worried.

All of a sudden, Vish felt… not scared, exactly, but something in that area. The man seemed defenseless, waiting by himself beside his ruined car with an unidentified enemy somewhere out there. He hesitated, then made the offer. "I could wait with you."

The man looked at him, his expression blank, and for a moment Vish thought he'd said something to offend him. Then he nodded. "Sure. If you wouldn't mind. Thanks. I was getting bored." He slammed down the hood and boosted himself up onto it. "Grab a seat."

Vish hesitated. "I don't want to destroy any fingerprints."

"Doesn't matter. Destroy away. I'm not going to report this."

Vish sat on the hood next to him. The car looked clean—shiny and freshly waxed, in fact—and if the man could trust his expensive suit to it, Vish didn't need to fret too much about getting his cheap work slacks dirty. "You really don't know who did this?"

"I can think of a few possibilities. A lot of people don't like me."

"I don't know who you are," Vish said. "It seems like I should, but I don't."

"No reason you should. Our social circles probably haven't overlapped much." The man extended a hand. "I'm Sparky."

16

"Vish." They shook.

"Fish?" Sparky asked. "Like… fish?" He made a little swimming motion with his hand.

"Vish. With a 'v'."

"Short for?" Sparky's expression was sharp, like it mattered.

"Viswanathan."

Sparky smiled. "I was hoping for Vicious. Or maybe Vishnu," he said. "Viswanathan? Isn't that a last name?"

"It's my mother's maiden name. Actually, it's my middle name, but I don't like my given name."

"Which is?"

"Michael."

Sparky stared at him as if he was trying to decide if Vish was making fun of him. It was an expression Vish saw a lot. Then he shook his head.

"So it's been established you're not an actor. Proceeding on the assumption you're not a career caterer, either, I'm guessing you're the other one." Off Vish's confused look, he elaborated: "Writer."

"Ah. Yes. I am. Trying to be one, at least."

"Screenplays?"

"Yes. I've just started, though. I'm not sure I have the hang of it yet."

"How long have you been in L.A.?" Sparky asked.

"A year, almost. I moved out from New York. I was a contributing editor at an online literary magazine, but it folded last year."

"So you moved out here. To write screenplays."

Was there a note of scorn in his tone, or was Vish overly sensitive on the issue? "Yeah, pretty much. You're in the entertainment industry?"

"Here? Who isn't?" Sparky smiled. "I'm on the management end of things. Nothing terribly glamorous." He propped his elbows against the windshield of the car and leaned back, staring up at the moonless sky. "You have any scripts you're shopping around?"

Idle curiosity, or genuine interest? "Nothing I'm happy with. Mostly I'm trying to get my book published."

A quick glance over at him. "Agent?"

Vish paused. "Ah… not right now. I had one in New York, but it didn't work out."

"Tell me about your book," Sparky said. "Pitch it to me. Really sell me on it."

Crud. Vish hated this kind of thing. Talking about himself made him self-conscious enough. Talking himself up, trying to make himself sound exciting and compelling and dynamic, made his soul wither and die. He took a deep breath and tried to arrange his thoughts.

"It's fiction, though it's sort of loosely based on my mother's life. She passed away last year." Sparky made some faint sympathetic noise at this, but said nothing. Vish continued. "She grew up in India and came to the United States and became a cardiologist. My book begins right after she started her internship at a hospital in Detroit."

He warmed to his narrative, gaining confidence, adding more and more details. Sparky's expression showed reassuring interest; he nodded in the right spots, silently encouraging Vish to go on.

When Vish finished, there was an odd moment of silence. Sparky smiled at him. "Sounds awful," he said.

His tone was so polite and cheery that for a moment Vish thought he had misheard. Before he could say anything, Sparky continued. "I mean, it's probably good. Well-written, at least. You seem smart, and you have a good grasp of the basic components of a story, and I have no doubt you can string words together in a pleasing manner. But seriously, it sounds like something I'd need to be paid to read."

He didn't need to sound so chipper about it. Vish swallowed once. "Okay. Thank you," he said.

Sparky gave him a sidelong look. "That's not much of a defense," he said.

"If it's not your kind of book, it's not your kind of book. There's no sense in me arguing the point."

"You're doing this all wrong, you know." Another smile. "This is the part where you tell me why this *should* be my kind of book. Turn on the charm. Sell yourself. Flirt with me, if applicable. Because if you're at all perceptive, and I think you probably are, you've picked up on clues that I might be someone important."

"I've made a note of that, yes."

"So…?"

"So I'm not comfortable promoting myself, that's all."

"You're in the wrong industry, then," Sparky said. "Nothing ventured, nothing gained, right?"

"I've ventured. Believe me, I've ventured. And I've never gained, have never even come close to gaining. Nothing's ever come of anything I've tried, and I've always ended up feeling cheap and ridiculous for the effort." It came out a bit sharper than he'd intended. Hard to tell in the darkness, but he thought Sparky looked surprised.

"So what's the plan then, Vish?" A note of something new in Sparky's voice, something slinky and coy slithering in beneath the sardonic bonhomie. "Keep serving shitty food to the beautiful people at parties until a handsome stranger offers you fame and fortune on a silver tray?"

Ah. Sparky was playing with him. Sparky might also be kind of an asshole. He was bored and killing time, and he had nothing to give him. Vish almost smiled, suddenly more at ease. Assholes he could handle. "I suppose, if you're offering," he said. "Want to be my fairy godfather, Sparky?"

Another flash of those overlong incisors. Sparky was prettier when he didn't smile. "So you can flirt. I'd wondered." He sat upright. "Send me your book. I'll go through it, and we'll see what can be done."

"You already said you won't like it," Vish said. It came out a little bitchy.

"Doesn't matter. I don't have to like it. We'll do what we need to find a market for it." Sparky fished around in his wallet and produced a business card. He handed it to Vish. "That's my office. I'll be in on Monday."

Vish glanced at the card. Sparky Mother, it read, with a telephone number. No title, no company name. It also had a little line drawing on it, a fuzzy blue cartoon tiger holding a sparkler.

It was far and away the dumbest business card Vish had ever seen.

"Okay. Thanks," he said. He stuffed the card in his pants pocket. This was confusing. Was Sparky agreeing to take on his book, despite his clear antipathy toward it? What did he do, exactly? He'd said he was a manager… no, he'd said he was on the management side, which wasn't quite the same thing.

Sparky grinned. "You're not going to call me, are you?"

"I don't know," Vish said. "Maybe, maybe not. I don't know anything about you."

"So Google me. That's a good place to start. See what you think after that." Sparky shrugged. "I can do amazing things with you, if you've got the balls to let me."

Bit of a taunt there. Unmistakable. "We'll see."

"We surely will." Sparky nodded toward the curved road, where an approaching pair of headlights sliced through the darkness. "That's my ride."

A black sports car pulled onto the shoulder just ahead of them. Sparky slid off the hood of his own car and ambled over to the driver's side.

A tinted window rolled down. An Asian woman, Korean maybe, with bobbed copper hair and huge gold hoop earrings looked up at Sparky from underneath a thick sheaf of glossy bangs. "Hey, you," she said. "Hop in. They'll tow you in the morning."

"Thanks, Poppy. Poppy, this is Vish." Sparky beckoned him over. "He was nice enough to keep me company, I figure the least we can do is give him a ride home." He turned to Vish. "Where do you live?"

Poppy glanced at Vish. She was extremely pretty and extremely made-up. Eyes lined in a thick layer of smudgy black, lashes long and spiky. She wore a gold tank dress covered in large sequins that glittered when she moved.

While Sparky's attention was on Vish, she caught his eye and shook her head, just a fraction of an inch, once.

Ah. "Don't worry about it," Vish said. "The bus is fine. Thanks anyway."

Sparky frowned. "You sure?" he asked. "We can at least run you down the hill to your bus stop."

"I need the walk," Vish said. He'd grown a little cold sitting in the night air with Sparky, and his white button-down shirt and the dumb red polyester vest Jamie made all her employees wear so they'd look like a cohesive team weren't providing much warmth. A ride would be nice, actually, but Poppy had sent him a very clear signal he shouldn't take Sparky up on his offer. "Hollywood isn't far from here."

"Suit yourself," Sparky said. He stuck out his hand. "Good meeting you, Vish. And thanks."

"Sure." They shook. Sparky's nails were manicured; the white cuff that stuck out from beneath his suit coat was crisp and immaculate. Diamond cufflinks glittered.

"Call me Monday, right? We'll talk," Sparky said. He sauntered around the front of the car and slid into the passenger seat.

With a quick nod at Vish, Poppy pulled forward, flipped a u-turn in the middle of the road, and headed down the hill.

Vish followed at a slow walk. As soon as Poppy's car rounded the first turn, the lights from the taillights vanished, leaving him alone in the dark.

CHAPTER THREE

IT TOOK JUST over two hours to reach his apartment. A slow and mostly empty bus through Hollywood, an interminable wait at a grim, lonely stop on the wrong end of Fairfax, another bus down Venice Boulevard all the way to the ocean. A foggy night here, colder and clammier than it had been in the hills.

His apartment was stuffy. Vish yanked open the windows. He should get some sleep—he had to open the shop at nine tomorrow, and it was now past two—but he felt wound up, almost jittery. He put on the kettle for a cup of chamomile tea and booted up his laptop.

Sparky Mother. Vish took out the absurd business card and stared at it. Time to figure out who he was, what power he wielded in the industry, what services he could provide for Vish, what kind of fairy godfather he could be.

A Google search. The electronic data trail would give him a starting point: the deals he made, the press he received, the company he kept.

One result.

Vish frowned. That was a mistake. Had to be. Even the lowest-level agent or producer or assistant had more of an online presence than that. Vish himself had dozens of search results for his name, as a few guilty vanity Googles had shown.

The articles he'd written, his profiles on various social networking sites, a long-abandoned and frankly embarrassing attempt at a personal website… Vish had all that linked to his name, and Vish was nobody.

He looked at the single result. He wasn't familiar with the URL—some site called AgentProwl—but it looked relevant. He clicked on the link.

A message board. Aspiring actors swapping gossip about agents, or trying to find agents, or complaining about the agents they already had. He found the right thread, which was about six weeks old, started by someone posting under the optimistic screen name FutureStarr. Under the header *"Anyone know Sparky Mother?"*:

Hey I met this cute guy at the restaurant where I waitress today and when I mentioned I was an actress he gave me his card and said call him. He said he was an agent I think? I don't know he seemed legit but then I went to Google him and nobody knows anything about him so it seems kind of weird so does anyone know who he is because I REALLY need an agent and he seemed REALLY interested in me but now I'm thinking he just wanted to get into my pants (or rape me and stab me and dump my body in the hills LOL). His name is Sparky Mother I dont know what agency hes with and I dont want to call him until I know more. Plz help thx.

One response, from one month ago, from a user named DiegoXG:

Sparky Mother ruined my life.

Huh. That was it. That was the end of the electronic breadcrumb trail. Vish sat back and stared at the screen.

DiegoXG, whoever he was, wasn't going to be any more help than that. Vish clicked on his user name and found he'd joined the AgentProwl site just to post that single message. No other posts, no personal information linked to his profile, nothing.

It didn't make sense. Sparky had been at the party, and the guests obviously knew who he was. The bumblebee girl, the *Interstellar Boys* actress, she was on close terms with him and she was famous, or something close to famous. He seemed legitimate, just from the little Vish had talked with him. He even had a shadowy, vengeful enemy. By Hollywood standards, wasn't that a clear indication of his bona fides?

Maybe he went by a different name professionally, business card notwithstanding. In any case, "Sparky" had to be a nickname. Nobody named their kid Sparky. Vish stared at the card.

Sparky had said this was his office number. He wasn't in his office tonight. He'd be at home by now, or out with his glamorous friend Poppy. If Vish called now, he'd reach his voicemail, and maybe there'd be some clue there—the name of his company, his full name, something.

Vish took out his phone. Took a deep breath. Dialed the number on the stupid business card.

It didn't ring. It didn't connect. On the other end of the line, Vish heard a series of muted electronic clicks, like the phone company was trying its best to establish a connection but falling short. The clicks stopped, replaced by a dull echoing pulse, the sound rising and falling like distant waves rolling onto the shore.

Vish hung on the line for longer than necessary, listening to that electronic void, waiting to see if the call would go through. It didn't.

So Sparky's line was down. No big deal. Maybe he'd try again on Monday morning. Maybe he wouldn't.

He couldn't quite explain why, but he felt a surge of relief that he hadn't accepted the ride home from Sparky.

The earthquake struck at just before five in the morning. Vish was in the middle of a half-formed dream, something about yellow-eyed coyotes feasting on the broken-doll corpse of the girl in the bumblebee dress, when an enormous jolt shattered him into consciousness. He opened his eyes in time to see a dazzling array of blue-white sparks bursting skyward, fireworks-style, from the power lines outside his bedroom window, then everything went black.

Small, staccato jolts followed the first big one. In the moments between the jolts, the floor rocked and swayed and slid. His bed was on wheels, rolling across the deck of a ship bobbing in a storm. Ah, yes, his very first earthquake. A rite of passage for living in Los Angeles.

Something crashed in his living room. There were smaller thunks, too, and a loud rattle. Was someone twisting his doorknob, trying to get into his apartment? It took a moment to realize it was just the windows shaking in their frames.

Just under twenty seconds of motion and chaos, then stillness returned. Vish remained in bed.

Adrenaline raced through his body, though he'd neither fought nor fled. He'd been frozen in place, his brain too

27

overwhelmed to settle upon a single course of action. Brilliant survival instincts. Top notch.

He sat up. Pulled his wits together. Swung his legs out of bed. His knees were so shaky he could barely stand at first. Outside his bedroom window, all was darkness under that moonless sky.

He left the relative safety of his bedroom. Moving gingerly, padding barefoot, proceeding with care. At the entrance to his living room, he whacked his shin and almost fell across... was that his coffee table? Really? A huge, heavy slab of pressed laminate material, it had somehow wedged itself in the doorway. Vish tried to shove it aside, but it wouldn't budge. He crawled over it on hands and knees.

A flashlight would be useful. He had one in the junk drawer in his kitchen, probably. It had batteries in it, but they hadn't been changed since he moved here. He navigated his way through the living room by touching the wall, then groped his way along the kitchen counter until he located the junk drawer. Under matchbooks and takeout menus, there it was, his flashlight. And hey, it even worked! It was a tiny thing, pocket-sized, and it emitted a feeble, watery slice of urine-colored light, but right now it was the only source of illumination in the apartment. In all of the city, it seemed.

He shone it around. Things looked okay. One of his cupboard doors had flown open, but the contents—two juice glasses, two plates, a coffee mug—had remained in place. His windows hadn't broken. The building hadn't cracked in two, the second level hadn't come crashing down into the ground floor.

Everything wobbled. Vish reached out toward the closest wall to brace himself, but the aftershock stopped at once. Just a little reminder of what had just happened, just a little something to get his heart racing again.

Noises. A police siren somewhere, a baby screaming from the apartment next door, where Mariposa lived with her mother. He'd heard the baby off and on for the past couple of weeks, the sound of its wails carrying through the cracker-thin walls. Right now it was howling, a harsh, scratchy, full-throated sound. Didn't sound good.

Vish slept in sweat pants and an old t-shirt. Under the circumstances, he looked presentable enough. With the aid of the flashlight, he located his flip-flops by the front door and slipped them on.

Pitch blackness outside, the stars obscured by the thick fog rolling in off the ocean. Only a single pinpoint of light in the sky, an airplane en route to nearby LAX. He groped for the railing that ran the length of the second level and squinted in the darkness. The damp ocean air smelled of seaweed, undercut with asphalt and exhaust.

The baby howled again. Vish rapped his knuckles on the door to the left of his apartment. "Mariposa? It's Vish, from next door. Are you and your mom okay?"

Raised female voices from inside, a flurry of Spanish, and then the door flew open. Vish instinctively pointed the flashlight at Mariposa's face, then realized he was blinding her and lowered it.

"Hey, you. Yeah, we're good." Mariposa wore a pink camisole that stopped several inches above her navel and a tiny, low-slung pair of lavender boxer shorts. After one quick glance down, Vish made sure to keep his eyes on her face. "Luis is being loud, but he's just dumb. He's fine."

Vish glanced over her shoulder, straining to see into the dark apartment. Under the baby's screams, he could hear a radio tuned to a Spanish-language station. Sounded like a news report. "Luis is the baby?" he asked.

Mariposa nodded. "My nephew. Little idiot. Mama's taking care of him for a while until my brother and his wife move into their new home." She rolled her eyes. "I bet he's been driving you crazy, right? Join the club. I swear, babies suck so much."

From somewhere inside the apartment, someone Vish couldn't see—Mariposa's mother, presumably—rattled off some quick Spanish. Judging by the clear note of warning in her tone, it was probably something about how her nubile teen daughter shouldn't chat in the doorway with an adult male neighbor while wearing only her skimpy nightclothes.

Mariposa glanced back and replied in Spanish, her tone that of exasperated teens everywhere. She turned back to Vish. "Have you been listening to the news? They said it was a four-point-seven. That's not very big." She sounded disappointed. "They think it was centered in Pacific Palisades, so that's why we felt it so bad here."

"Any word on damage?" Vish asked.

Mariposa shook her head. "Don't know. I heard a big crack, though. Right when it first happened. Didn't you?"

"A crack? Like, here in the building?"

Mariposa nodded. "Yeah. It was real loud. I think the stairs broke or something. You didn't hear it?"

"I don't think so. I can check it out for you, though."

"I'll go with you," Mariposa said. She stepped forward, fully intent on accompanying him in her tiny shorts and, he now saw, her gigantic fuzzy slippers.

Her mother said something again, her tone sharper and more pointed. Mariposa huffed out an impatient sigh and looked ready to argue, so Vish headed it off at the pass. "Why don't you stay with your mom and Luis? They could probably use you right now. I'll look around and let you guys know if there's anything you should be worried about."

Mariposa looked unhappy at this, but she didn't argue. "Whatever, I guess. Thanks for checking on us." She smiled. "You're a good neighbor, you know? I'm glad you didn't get hurt or nothing."

"Thanks. You, too. Glad everyone's okay."

Flashlight in hand, Vish headed toward the staircase leading down to the courtyard. He bobbed the pallid beam of light along the ground and the walls as he went. No cracks.

Everything was silent, punctuated only by the occasional angry wail from Luis upstairs. Fourteen units total in the building, seven on each floor. Mariposa was the only neighbor he knew by name. A couple units were unoccupied. Maybe more than a couple, actually; he'd seen several soon-to-be-former tenants hauling their stuff out of their apartments over the past year, but he hadn't seen anyone hauling stuff back in.

The gate to the low, rusty fence around the swimming pool stood wide open. That'd be a dangerous child hazard, if the pool were filled with water. As it happened, it was filled with furniture—three-legged end tables, dressers with missing drawers, a sofa with the cushions slashed and the stuffing hemorrhaging out, all souvenirs of past residents.

An argument could be made that his cramped East Village apartment had been kind of crappy, too. Silverfish that swarmed up from the tub drain, a warped bathroom door that refused to close all the way, a subtle stink of cat piss that intensified on humid days, even though he'd never owned a cat. He'd waged war on the smell, wielding bleach and scouring pads and all manner of industrial-strength cleansers, but had never managed to completely eradicate it. So it wasn't like he'd downgraded his situation much by moving out west, really.

He shone the flashlight around the base of the complex. Aha. The corner closest to the street had cracked and crumbled away, creating a foot-high jagged gap. Vish directed the beam inside the hole and saw coiled chicken wire in the space beneath the thin stucco exterior. Stucco over chicken wire. Everything considered, it was lucky the entire structure hadn't collapsed when the earth moved.

A short scream sliced through the night. Female, probably, and it sounded like it'd been abruptly cut off. Vish froze and listened. His heartbeat quickened.

That had come from just outside the front gate. He hurried out to the sidewalk and swooped his flashlight in all directions. The beam didn't penetrate more than a foot or two through the fog.

He cleared his throat. "Is anyone here?" he asked. "Do you need help?"

Nothing but silence. "Hello?" His voice sounded thin and muted in the fog. He hesitated, keeping still, listening for any response.

Everything was quiet. He was alone. After hesitating a moment longer, heart pounding, muscles still on high alert, he turned back to his apartment building.

In the darkness, his sandaled foot struck a sprinkler head jutting up from the patch of lawn just outside the security gate. He pitched forward and hit the sidewalk, the pain of impact jolting through his hands and knees.

The flashlight went out upon contact with the cement. Vish remained on all fours for a moment, conducting a quick internal diagnostic check. Nothing was broken. His knees hurt and his palms were scraped, but it all seemed minor.

He rose to his feet and brushed off his pants, and that was when the back of his head exploded.

CHAPTER FOUR

SOMEBODY HIT ME. *Somebody actually hit me.*

The cold roughness of cement against his cheek, a curiously dull and imprecise pain across the entire back of his skull, like a nascent headache that couldn't commit to forming. Had he lost consciousness? Had time passed—minutes, or even hours—since someone had crept up behind him in the darkness and bashed him over the head? Or had he only been momentarily stunned by the blow, and even now someone was waiting nearby, watching him, readying for a repeat assault?

He froze in place, sprawled facedown on the sidewalk, and organized his thoughts against the mounting wave of adrenaline-fueled panic. He was okay. He was alone, he was pretty sure he was alone, because surely if someone was planning on hitting him again, they would have done it by now.

He got to his feet. Carefully, delicately, bones protesting every move. He couldn't see anything, he'd lost the flashlight, but the world around him swirled and shifted with his every movement. Standing upright was a minor triumph.

The top of his head grazed something, which sent another spike of panic through him, until it dawned on him what it was. A low-hanging branch from the quince tree out front, a branch he ducked under every day on his walk to work. He reached up and touched it, the feel of the bark reassuring under his fingertips. Okay, then. He hadn't been attacked. In the darkness, he'd risen too fast, bonked his head on the branch, and knocked himself out.

He moved toward his building, shuffling his feet against the sidewalk to avoid tripping again, hands outstretched. He touched the security gate, iron and chipped paint beneath his fingers. He hadn't shut it all the way when he'd hurried in the direction of the scream, which was good, because… crap, the pockets of his sweatpants were empty, which meant he'd lost his keys when he fell. With a sinking feeling, he navigated his way up the stairs to the second floor.

He hadn't locked his apartment door when he'd gone to check on Mariposa. Good news. He wouldn't be spending the night on the disemboweled sofa in the swimming pool. He'd look for his keys as soon as it was light outside…

There was someone in his living room.

Someone was sitting in the armchair against the far wall. Even without any light, he could see his—her?—silhouette, an almost imperceptibly denser blackness than the blackness of his living room. Vish froze in the doorway.

"Who are you?" he asked.

No response. No movement.

He was an idiot. There was no one in his apartment, just like no one had attacked him. Nothing more than a trick of the shadows. Still, it took him a moment, kind of a long moment, before he summoned enough nerve to walk to the armchair, extend a (trembling, maybe) hand into the darkness to touch the upholstered chair back, and confirm no one was there.

Yeah, he was an idiot. Nothing more than that. It'd been a long, strange night, and his imagination was running amuck. His head hurt, he was deeply confused, and he had to be at work in a few hours. He went to bed.

CHAPTER FIVE

THE POWER WAS still out when the sun rose, but at least now he could see, which was a huge improvement. The coffee table still blocked the path to the living room, but he shoved it back into place, picked up a handful of scattered letters and magazines, closed the cupboards, and returned a toppled lamp to its rightful position. Good as new.

His keys were on the end table by the door, right where they should be. In the darkness and confusion following the quake, he hadn't taken them with him when he went to check on his neighbors.

His head still hurt, damn it all. A buzzing in the back of his brain, a dull background noise that made it hard to think straight. Nothing too acute, but plenty annoying.

The gas had shut off automatically during the quake, which meant there was no hot water, so Vish couldn't shower or shave. He splashed his face in the bathroom sink and called it good. There was a little dried blood crusted on his hair; when he dabbed at his scalp with a damp washcloth, he discovered the skin had broken where he'd bonked his head.

At least his cell phone was working. Vish considered for a moment, then called Kate.

She answered on the first ring. Lucky day. Vish hadn't talked to his sister in a couple of weeks. Between her new baby and her work schedule, pinning her down long enough to have a decent conversation required luck or patience.

"Hey, Vish. What's up?" Bad connection. Her voice was distant and had an echo, like she was speaking from the end of a tunnel.

"Can you talk? You sound far away," Vish said.

"I am far away." He heard the amusement in her voice, bouncing off of satellites from Boston to Los Angeles. Kate was a gastroenterologist, deeply entrenched in a rigorous and hard-won internship at Mass General. Vish felt feeble and marginal in comparison to her radiant intellect and formidable accomplishments. "I'm in the car. I have you on speaker. I can give you maybe four minutes until I reach the hospital."

"We had an earthquake last night," Vish said.

"You did? A big one? I didn't see anything online before I left."

"Might not have made national news. It felt big to me, but I don't have anything to compare it to."

"Are you okay?" Kate asked. "Did anything break?"

"Everything's fine. Stuff fell, but it was no big deal. The power's still out." He paused, considering his words, knowing this would scare her. "I bumped my head in the dark."

"Really? How?" Kate asked. Yeah, he was right, that was alarm in her voice. "Did you get it checked out?"

"It's not worth checking out. It wasn't really anything."

"Don't mess around with a head injury, Vish. You know better than that. If your brain swells up—"

"I could die. Yes. I know. It's not going to swell up," he said. "I'm fine. I shouldn't have mentioned it."

A long pause, thick with background traffic noises. "Did you tell dad about the quake yet?"

"I'll email him when the power comes back. He's probably going to bed now. They're fourteen hours ahead of me, right?"

"Call him anyway. He won't care if you wake him. He'd like to hear your voice. I think he's lonely."

"He shouldn't be. He's got plenty of family there to keep him company." It sounded snottier than he'd intended. Their father had moved back to his birthplace last year to immerse himself in the warm, comforting nest of his brothers and sisters, their offspring and grandchildren, his aged but still healthy parents. It had been the best possible balm for his vast, encompassing grief. Only a uniquely uncharitable son would begrudge him that bit of comfort.

"He misses mom." There was a faint reprimand in Kate's tone.

"Don't we all?" Bitchy. That was bitchy. Vish dialed back the reflexive defensiveness. "Maybe I'll try calling him tonight. I have to work this morning."

"How are you doing for money?" Kate asked.

"Fine. It's all good," he said.

"You sure?"

"Yeah. The job's going pretty well. Jamie's been giving me a lot of extra hours."

There was another pause on Kate's end. "Vish, are you happy there?"

"Sure, sometimes," he said. "Maybe not today. I don't think I like earthquakes."

"Los Angeles still seems like the wrong city for you," she said. "You can publish your book from anywhere. I know New York didn't work out all that well, but if you've given up on the idea of screenwriting, you could always move here—"

"Thanks, Kate." He had a sudden urge to tell her about Sparky Mother, the big-league Hollywood agent (manager?) who was keenly interested in his book, just so he'd seem a little less pathetic, then reconsidered. Kate had a finely-calibrated bullshit detector, and his story wouldn't stand up to pointed questions. He cleared his throat. "Look, I need to get ready for work. We'll email, right?"

"Of course. Take care of yourself, Vish. See someone about that head injury." The call disconnected without warning. Even in the midst of her concern about her aimless and floundering baby brother, Kate rarely had time to wrap up conversations gracefully.

A dull pain in his gut to match the one in his head. He was too old to feel this homesick. He *was* home, here in Los Angeles, and if he was somewhat less than happy, it was his own fault. He was an adult, wholly capable of carving out his own rich, satisfying, fulfilling life. Even if it didn't always seem like it.

The sun was out in force, burning off the last of the fog that had rolled in during the night. Saturday mornings were never bustling in Venice. Today, in the aftermath of the quake, it seemed even quieter than usual.

The power must be back, at least in places. The streetlights were operating; traffic flowed as it should. There were a few cars on the road, signs of the city waking up and returning to life, though Vish was the only pedestrian. He felt exposed, examined, under scrutiny from unseen observers.

The static in his head did weird things to his thoughts, lending credence to Kate's worries about his brain. Sometimes he could almost see someone walking beside him, a shadowy figure matching pace with him, visible only out of the very corners of his eyes. A figure that vanished whenever he turned his head.

Stupid. A flight of fancy, brought about by an eventful evening and not nearly enough sleep. If he could make it through the day, he could crawl onto his creaky futon, burrow under his scratchy comforter, and not rise until Monday. It was a good thought.

Jamie's shop was on Abbot Kinney. A freshly-painted blue storefront with crisp white awnings, as precious and picturesque as a cottage in the English countryside, wedged in between a tattoo parlor and a bicycle repair shop. "Comestibles" was scribbled in curly gold letters above the door. Though the bulk of Jamie's revenue came from catering gigs, they sold coffee and pastries and sandwiches to walk-in customers.

Here, the power was still out. Vish flipped the fuses in the back of the store, just to be certain, then called Jamie.

"Crapola," Jamie said as soon as Vish filled her in. "Power's been down the whole time? We only lost it for maybe twenty minutes here in Brentwood." She thought for a moment. "It's been more than four hours since the quake. That means everything has to be tossed. Food service rules."

"The refrigerator hasn't been opened. Everything in there will still be cold," Vish said.

"Doesn't matter. Even if the power comes back right now, I can't risk it. Just lock up and go home. I'll come in tomorrow and toss everything."

She sounded glum. Vish couldn't blame her. "Want me to do it?"

"Thanks, sugar, but I'll need to do an inventory. How bad was the quake where you were?"

"Alarming," Vish said.

"Weird. We barely felt it here. It woke me up, but that's about it."

After a few more commiserating words, he hung up. As badly as he felt about Jamie's ruined inventory, the prospect of going home early was a relief. His head still hurt, and he still felt weird, overexposed. He needed rest, safe in his apartment, protected from the outside world.

The shop door opened. A young woman in a baggy sweater and leggings stepped into the dark store. She had a pointy chin and a dainty curve of a nose, with a shiny helmet of chin-length reddish-blonde hair. She removed her oversized sunglasses, glanced up at the lights, and smiled at Vish. "No power?"

"No. Sorry. I was just getting ready to close up," he said.

She winced. "I was supposed to stop in this morning for a tasting? I'm throwing a tea party next Saturday."

Jamie had mentioned that yesterday. "Right. I'm sorry. Would it be possible to reschedule?"

She hovered in the doorway. "Not really. This is my only free morning. Can we do it right now? The lady I talked to last week said everything would be pre-made, right?"

"It's all ready, but..." He shook his head. "It's been in the refrigerator, and the power's been down since the earthquake. I can't serve you anything."

"It'd still be cold, though." She smiled. No makeup, clear skin, small white teeth. She had a tiny mouth like a peach satin bow. "It'll be fine. I won't get food poisoning. Or if I do, it'll be my own fault."

"I really can't—"

She stepped further into the shop. "Please? It would be a huge help. I'd really appreciate it."

It wasn't his call. Jamie had said to close up, and this was Jamie's shop. But this woman seemed friendly, and she was very pretty, and that was a debilitating combination. He took a deep breath, then nodded.

"Sure. Okay. Just give me a minute." He disappeared into the kitchen and opened the fridge. The light didn't come on, but a reassuring blast of cold air flooded out of it, which chased away any lingering worries that he was about to poison this friendly, pretty stranger. Right in front was a little white box with "TROY" scrawled on top in Jamie's curly handwriting.

He returned to the main room of the shop and held up the box. "Are you Troy?"

"That's me." She seated herself on one of the high stools at the front counter. Vish arranged the contents of the box on a doily-lined porcelain plate. A lemon-rosemary tart, a cocoa meringue kiss, a caramel *petit four*, a passion-fruit *macaron*, a puff filled with lavender custard and topped with a crystallized violet. After giving up on her dreams of film stardom, Jamie had trained, and trained well, under a pastry chef in San Francisco.

"Normally I'd serve you tea or coffee with this, but…" He shrugged. "No hot water. Sorry about that."

Troy nibbled on the side of the *petit four*. "No worries. Oh, yum," she said. "Oh, that's fantastic. Wow."

She set it down and picked up the tart. She took mouse-like nibbles from each pastry in turn, tiny teeth flashing, not eating any treat in its entirety, even though they were scarcely more than a bite apiece. Vish hovered behind the counter and tried not to stare at her too openly. She was lovely, in a way that stood out even in beauty-glutted Los Angeles, luminous yet unfussy.

"Fantastic," she said at last. "Everything. Just as it is." She looked up at Vish. "Are we set for Saturday, or do you need anything else from me?"

"I'm not sure. Let me make sure Jamie has your information," Vish said. Jamie kept her events schedule tacked to the back wall. He turned away from Troy.

She inhaled sharply, almost a gasp. When she spoke, her voice sounded funny. "Do you know you're bleeding?"

He brought his hand up to the back of his head, which was damp with fresh blood from the cut on his scalp. A few drops had drizzled down the back of his neck and stained the collar of his shirt, which was probably what alarmed Troy. "Excuse me," he said.

He headed to the small bathroom in back. No windows, no lights, so he kept the door open while he ran water over a wad of paper towels.

As he wiped away the blood, Troy popped her head through the doorway. She held up a dishtowel, which she must have pilfered from behind the front counter. "Here," she said. "Let me."

She wedged herself into the tiny room, sliding around the sink to get closer to him. Vish turned his back to her and let her dab at the cut. This close, he could smell her perfume, some mixture of grapefruit and thyme, both astringent and comforting. At her touch, his headache felt a little better, and the static in his brain receded. "What'd you do to yourself?" she asked.

"It's silly. I bumped my head when I was exploring in the dark after the earthquake," he said.

Troy clucked sympathetically. "That's why your pupils look funny," she said. "At first I thought you might be high, but you didn't seem like the type."

"My pupils look funny?" Vish checked himself out in the mirror. Huh. His pupils seemed their usual size. Maybe a little on the small side. Hard to tell in the dim light.

"You might have a concussion," Troy said. "You should get this looked at."

"No, I'm fine," Vish said. "It looks more serious than it is. Scalp wounds always bleed a lot. I just have a very mild headache, that's all."

"Humor me," Troy said. "Let me take you to the hospital. You shouldn't mess around with a head injury."

She sounded so much like Kate that Vish had to smile. "No, really, it's nothing to worry about. Thank you," he said. He paused. "In any case, I don't have health insurance right now."

Embarrassing to admit that, coming as he did from a family of medical professionals. Troy just shrugged. "So they'll send you a bill. Sucks, but is it worth risking your life?" She placed a hand on his wrist. Her nails were short and unpolished. His skin tingled at her touch, as though some kind of energy passed between them, and he could feel himself starting to fall for her.

Kind-hearted pretty people. Vish went to jelly around kind-hearted pretty people every time.

"Come on. I'll help you close up, then I'll run you to the hospital to get you checked out. Okay?"

Somehow, almost against his will, Vish found himself following her to her car, a sporty gold two-seater. Compact yet glamorous, the perfect vehicle for Troy. She hauled an enormous leather shoulder bag filled with a wadded-up jacket and what looked like a stack of screenplays off of the passenger seat and shifted it to the floor. "Sorry if your legs get kind of scrunched. Hop in," she said.

Vish obeyed, even though he wished he could put a stop to this. Despite her mild, friendly appearance, she must have some force of will behind her, because he found himself following her without arguing. He didn't want to go to the hospital, now or ever. He felt fine, albeit a little groggy. Head was maybe a little sore, but not enough to warrant all this fuss and bother.

It seemed important to make Troy happy, though, so he leaned back in the passenger seat, closed his eyes, and let her take charge of his life.

CHAPTER SIX

TROY DROVE HIM to the big hospital on Venice Boulevard. From there, she was firmly in command. At her request, Vish forked over his driver's license and let her fill out his admission forms, let her steer him to a hard plastic seat beneath a wall-mounted television set in the waiting room, let her talk to the nurse at the front counter.

After too long of a wait, after Vish had explained to Troy once more that this was kind but unnecessary, because he felt perfectly fine, really, a willowy doctor with smooth brown skin and a crisp white smock finally led him into her examination room. She introduced herself as Doctor Gott. Vish blinked.

"Doctor… God?" he asked.

She didn't smile. "No relation. Gott, two Ts." She gestured for him to hop up on the table, then shone a pen light in his eyes. "What happened?"

"I hit my head on a tree branch."

She prodded at the back of his head, parting his hair with slim fingers. "Tree branch?" she asked. A hint of skepticism at the edges of her tone, maybe.

"Yeah. I was checking around my apartment building for damage after the quake, and I stood up too quickly and bonked my head."

Doctor Gott didn't say anything. Vish fought a wild compulsion to elaborate further. After a moment, she stepped back and smiled at him. "Well, let's get you checked out."

She shone more lights in his eyes and prodded at his skull, all while keeping up a calm patter and jotting down notes on her clipboard. Vish answered her questions as best he could. She dabbed at his bloody scalp with a mesh pad and applied some antibacterial ointment to the cut, then gave a small nod.

"Okay, Vish," she said. "Pupils look good, your reactions are normal, and that wound's not deep enough for stitches. Keep it clean, and you should be fine. To err on the side of caution, though, I'd like to order a CT scan, just to make sure there's no swelling on the brain."

Vish hesitated. "Is it necessary?"

"It's a good idea." She smiled at his reluctance. "It's not complicated, and it won't hurt a bit."

"I'm sure it won't. It's just…" He shrugged. "'CT scan' is a very expensive phrase."

She glanced down at his paperwork on her clipboard. She considered for a moment, then nodded once. "I do recommend it, but I can't force you to get one. Your choice. Promise me, though, that you'll return immediately if you feel dizzy or nauseous, or if you feel anything out of the ordinary at all."

"Great. Yes, of course. Thank you," Vish said.

"Keep awake for at least the next twelve hours, too. I'd advise having a friend stay with you. Ask Commander Hotpants if she's up to it." At Vish's look of complete incomprehension, she frowned. "Troy Van Ellen. I saw her with you in the waiting room. That was her, right?"

Vish didn't know Troy's last name, and he'd lost track of the conversation somehow, but he nodded. "Yeah, that's Troy."

"Good." Doctor Gott smiled. "Have her keep an eye on you. This is not a good day for being alone."

No sense explaining he'd only met Troy and thus she wouldn't be interested in babysitting him. He nodded, then hesitated. "Can I ask you something? When I said I bumped my head on a tree branch, you looked like you didn't believe me."

She considered. "The skin split cleanly. Something rough like a branch, you'd typically expect the scalp to look torn. Your injury is more consistent with a blow from something smooth, like a baton or a pipe." At his look of confusion, she shook her head. "But injuries are strange beasts sometimes. You say it was a branch, that's plausible. Just wanted to be sure someone hadn't beaten you up, that's all."

When he returned to the waiting room, Troy was deep in animated conversation with a pair of teen girls. She laughed at something they said, her red-gold hair managing to shimmer even under the flat glare of the fluorescent lights, then patted one of the girls on the shoulder and gave the other a quick one-armed hug. When she spotted Vish, she leaned forward and said something inaudible to them, which made them erupt into delighted giggles, then headed over to him.

"All clear?" she asked.

"Yeah. I'm fine," he said.

"Cool. Let me run you home," she said. She hoisted her purse onto her shoulder.

Vish hesitated. "Do I have to fill out any more paperwork or anything?"

"Nope. You're good to go." Troy took his elbow gently and led him to the door. She turned to wave goodbye to the girls one more time.

"Friends of yours?" Vish asked as they crossed through the parking lot.

"Ah... not really," she said.

Vish looked at her. Her face was flushed bright pink. Realization dawned. "You're famous, aren't you?"

She shook her head. "Hardly. But I'm on TV," she said. "It's this show on cable—*Interstellar Boys*?"

Ah. "Commander Hotpants? That what my doctor called you."

The pink deepened to crimson, though she looked pleased. "That's a nickname some fans have given my character. You'd have to see the show, but it makes sense in context."

Vish smiled. "I haven't seen it. Her comment confused me greatly."

Troy snorted. "I can imagine." She considered. "The show is the only big thing I've ever done, and not many people watch it. So, no, I'm definitely not famous. I'm surprised your doctor recognized me."

"I'm sure I'd like your show if I saw it. I've heard good things about it. I just don't have a television," Vish said. "I mean, right now I don't. I've had one in the past. I don't want it to sound like I'm anti-television or something."

Something about Troy—her pretty smile, maybe, or the light pressure of her small hand on his arm—turned him into a babbling idiot. She just grinned and led him to her car. "You're not missing much. I mean, it's a really good show, I'd say that even if I wasn't on it, but it's not going to change anyone's life. It's just cute and fun, that's all."

"One of your costars was at a party I catered last night." The girl in the bumblebee dress, teetering in heels on the railing, poised above oblivion. "I can't remember her name. Tiny blonde teenager, short hair?"

"Aw, Kelsey? You met Kelsey? Did you get to talk to her? She's a darling, isn't she? I adore her to pieces. The entire cast is so great, and we all get along so well. It makes going to work a pleasure."

Easy to believe. Impossible to picture anyone not getting along with Troy. "I didn't talk to her. But she seemed nice."

Troy smiled. "Where do you live?"

"About five blocks from here. Go straight down Venice."

"What did the doctor say? Do you have a concussion?"

"A small one, at the very worst. She didn't think it seemed too bad. I'm just supposed to stay awake for a while. Make sure I don't fall unconscious, I guess."

She gave him a sidelong look as she pulled out of the lot. "Do you need someone to stay with you?"

"She suggested that, but I don't think it's necessary."

She shrugged. "I don't have plans. We could hang out, if you wanted."

Funny how just those casual words made his heart beat a little faster. "That'd be great," Vish said. "I'd love the company. But please don't feel obligated in any way. I'm really fine."

"No problem. I'd feel terrible if you slipped into a coma while you were by yourself," Troy said. "Which way on Venice?"

"Left. You'll be taking another left on Glencoe."

Her expression was neutral as she looked at his building. Too neutral. Vish was practical enough not to be ashamed of where he lived. This was what he could afford, this sufficed for his needs. Seeing it through her eyes, though, was different. The rusting fence, the discarded furniture in the empty pool...

She brightened once they were inside his apartment. "Oh, this is nice," she said. "You have really good style."

"Thank you." He *did* have good style. He'd painted the walls when he first moved in, covering the tobacco-yellowed white in pale olive with a painstaking ivory border at the top to lend the illusion of crown molding. Glossy black paint over pasteboard bookcases, a chenille slipcover over his Goodwill couch, acrylic rugs in Persian-inspired patterns over the gray nylon carpet.

"Are you hungry?" she asked.

Which is how they ended up sitting on the couch together, Troy mere inches away from him, pizza box on the coffee table. She had taken charge of ordering. The pizza was cheeseless and meatless, which was fine, if not Vish's first choice. If the food was bland, the company was more than worth it. Troy was an easy conversationalist, both talkative and attentive. If there was anything she'd rather be doing on her weekend than sitting around with some stranger while making sure his brain didn't spontaneously hemorrhage, she showed no sign of it. She asked questions about his life, lots of questions, and seemed genuinely fascinated by his answers.

"So what have you written?" she asked.

"A lot of short stories. Two novels. A few relentlessly mediocre screenplays." Vish swallowed a bite of pizza. It had artichoke hearts and sun-dried tomatoes on it. It was okay. Add little goat cheese and maybe some crispy pancetta, and it'd be downright tasty. "Back in New York, coming out here and writing screenplays sounded like a good idea, but as soon as I got here… I don't know. I don't think I have a feel for this industry."

"Do you have an agent?" she asked.

Vish shook his head. "I did in New York. She couldn't interest anyone in my writing, so she dropped me."

Troy winced in sympathy. "Rough. You're in good company, though. I know a lot of talented people, writers and actors, who haven't been able to get anywhere here. I've been lucky, I know. Right place, right time."

She plucked a kalamata olive off her pizza slice and ate it, her tongue flicking out to lick her fingers. "You should email me some of your stuff. I could pass it along to my agent. My agency represents writers, too. They're really good."

"Wow. Thank you. That would be very nice of you." Between Troy and Sparky, he'd had as many offers to read his material in the past day as in the entire year since he'd moved to Los Angeles.

That was a thought. "Do you know anyone named Sparky Mother?"

Troy frowned. Faint creases emerged on her forehead. Small lines around her eyes, too. She was probably a couple years older than Vish, though she looked good for any age. "Yeah, maybe. Is he an agent?"

Vish felt a surge of surprise. He'd almost written Sparky off as some kind of con artist. "Yeah, I think so. He might be a manager. I'm not really sure."

Troy nodded. "He's the one who used to throw all those big parties on Oscar night, isn't he? But I thought he died a while ago." She shook her head. "I might be thinking of the wrong guy."

"That can't be him. Sparky's young."

"Swifty. Swifty Lazar. That's who I was thinking of." Troy shrugged and shifted the conversation to other matters. Sparky was soon forgotten.

They whiled away the afternoon. They walked down to the water and strolled along the beach. They zipped to Santa Monica in Troy's little car and grabbed iced coffee on the Promenade. They saw a movie, something neither had much interest in seeing, something Vish forgot as soon as the end credits rolled. Troy insisted on paying for everything, quietly and politely but in a way that left no room for argument. Troy turned into a chipper and implacable brick wall whenever Vish tried to counter-insist on picking up the tab, rendering all his efforts useless.

Well, hell. She'd seen his shabby apartment, she knew he didn't have a car, she knew where he worked, she knew he didn't have health insurance… Later, as they were zipping back to his place, something dawned on him. "Back at the hospital, you didn't pay my bill, did you?"

She went pink again. "Actually, I did, yeah. It was easier that way."

"There's no need," he said. "Please. You can't do this. There's absolutely no reason you should pay for that."

"But I pressured you into going. And you don't have insurance." She smiled, somehow managing to seem both conciliatory and unrepentant. "Look, I don't mean to offend you, but I have an awful lot of money right now, and it's no big deal. Just let me do this for you, please. It makes everything so much smoother."

Vish exhaled, unsatisfied but not knowing how to push the point. "You're so *nice*," he said.

Troy giggled. "You make that sound like a bad thing."

"No. It's wonderful, and I'm so grateful to you. But you don't know me, and you've done so much for me today. I feel inadequate."

She glanced at him. "Don't," she said. "I want to do this. Don't think about it, don't worry about it, don't feel bad about it."

Vish leaned back against the headrest and watched the scenery, feeling like there was more he should say and not having the faintest idea how to say it.

CHAPTER SEVEN

VISH DIDN'T EXPECT to hear from Troy again. They'd exchanged email addresses before parting, and he'd dutifully sent her his novel, along with a quick message thanking her in advance for any help she could give him but making it clear nothing was expected. It'd taken him much too long to compose the note, to find the right balance: polite yet casual, interested but not creepy.

Two days later, he returned home from Comestibles and found Troy parked in front of his building. She slipped out of her car and fell into step with him as he approached the gate. "Vish! Sorry for just stopping by, but I wanted to let you know I read your book. I stayed up most of an entire night finishing it," she said. "I passed it along to Greg at my agency, and he's forwarded it to the literary desk, though it'll probably take a while before they get to it. But I thought it was wonderful."

"Thank you," Vish said. He glanced at her. She seemed sincere. Then again, she was an actress. "Thank you very much."

"So here's the thing," she said. She was turning pink again. "I also gave it to Freddie—Freddie Halterman, he's the guy who created *Interstellar Boys*, and he's brilliant and awesome—and I told him about you and how good your book is and how you're looking for work..."

She stopped. Vish's heartbeat picked up a little. "Oh?"

"Yeah, and he's really interested in meeting you. He said he looked through your book, I'm sure he hasn't had a chance to read it all the way yet, but I know he was totally impressed with your writing. I also know he wants to add more staff writers. I can't say for sure that's what he's going to offer you, and I don't want to get your hopes up, but he said to tell you he'd be interested in meeting you."

"Wow. Troy, thank you." Absurd to think the creator of a television series might offer a writing job to an unknown, but maybe Troy's opinion carried a lot of weight. "That's great news."

"I thought we could have dinner. To celebrate." She hoisted a bulging mesh bag. "I stopped at the farmers market. You might have plans already." She shrugged. "If not, I thought it might be fun to cook together."

He hesitated, caught off guard by her enthusiasm. Troy's brow wrinkled. "I come on strong, I know. I'm like this whenever I make a new friend. Some people get annoyed by me." She smiled. "If you've got things to do, or if you'd just rather not, it's no big deal, really. I won't take offense."

"No, not at all. I'm glad you stopped by. Cooking dinner sounds like fun." He held open the front gate. "Come in."

The crumbled hole in the corner of the building was still there, unfixed. Someone must've inspected it at some point, because now there was an orange safety cone in front.

When they reached the top of the stairs, the neighboring door opened. Mariposa peeked out. "Hey, Vish," she said. She looked at Troy with frank interest. "Who's that?"

"Hi, Mariposa. Mariposa, this is my friend Troy."

"Nice to meet you, Mariposa. I really like your sandals. Those are cute." Troy smiled at her, all dimples and charm.

Mariposa was immune to Troy's dimples. She looked her over, up and down, and gave her a cool nod. "Thanks." She shifted her attention back to Vish. "Do you know who's moving in beneath you? I haven't seen anyone, but they've been making tons of noise all day. Bumps and thumps."

"I don't know," Vish said. "Good that the building's filling up, I guess. It's been kind of weird with no one around."

"I know. It's creepy." Mariposa glanced back into her apartment. "I'm alone with Luis, so I better go."

"Nice meeting you," Troy said. Mariposa ducked back inside without answering. As soon as the door was closed, Troy grinned at Vish. "She has a crush on you."

Vish snorted. "I seriously doubt that," he said. He fumbled to unlock his own door, hoping Mariposa wasn't eavesdropping.

"Are you kidding me? She came outside as soon as she heard us coming. And she really scoped out her competition. Did you see the stink-eye she gave me?"

"She might've felt shy. Maybe she recognized you."

Troy shrugged and moved past him into his apartment. "Maybe. Doesn't mean she's not sweet on you. Is the idea really so crazy?"

"Yes. Yes, it is. For starters, I'm too old for her to even consider me that way."

"That's probably part of the appeal. You're old enough that her mother would wig out at the idea of you as her boyfriend, which makes it kind of fun and dangerous, but at the same time you're sweet and gentle and bunny-rabbit cute, which neutralizes any real threat. That combination is catnip to teen girls. Trust me, I used to be an expert."

Vish raised his eyebrows. "Bunny-rabbit cute?"

"Oh, yes," Troy said. "Absolutely." She winked at him.

Was that good? Probably not—after all, she'd essentially just told him that she found him innocuous and kind of sexless. Did Troy like cute boys, or had she left that phase behind in her teen years? As Vish tried to work this out, she headed for the kitchen and plopped her mesh bag down on the counter. "This is going to sound like not much fun, but bear with me. I picked up tofu—it's the firm kind, not the drippy crap, and it's not bad at all if you cook it right—and then a bunch of vegetables and herbs and stuff. I thought we could do a stir-fry."

She was right. It didn't sound fun. "Sounds great. Healthy."

"Do you drink?" Troy pulled a bottle of red wine out of her bag. "And if you do, point me in the direction of your corkscrew."

Troy was a good cook. Troy, from what Vish had seen thus far, was probably good at everything she did. Vish had worked for Jamie long enough to be comfortable in a kitchen; he chopped vegetables to Troy's specifications, then watched as she cooked everything up with sesame oil and grated ginger and soy sauce. They drank while they cooked, the kitchen growing warm and filling with good smells.

At one point, Troy excused herself to use the bathroom. A few seconds later, Vish was startled by a loud yelp.

"Troy?" he asked.

She opened the door, giggling. "You have to see this." She beckoned him over. "I wanted to replace your toilet paper roll, so I checked under the sink," she said. She pointed at the open cabinet covering the pipes. "I'm guessing it's not usually like this?"

The back of the bathroom wall had crumbled away, revealing a jagged hole. The edges of the hole were coated with what Vish initially took to be some kind of puffy plastic insulation, until he noticed it was moving. Grubs. Huge, soft, pale grubs, dozens of them, clinging around the edges of the gap, climbing up out of the darkness and into Vish's apartment.

Vish wasn't squeamish, but the sight made him flinch. "God. Yuck. Sorry you had to find that," he said. "The wall must have crumbled during the earthquake."

"Do you have a maintenance guy?" Troy asked.

Vish shook his head. "The landlord lives in the building. I'll get him."

Troy insisted on coming with him. Vish wished she wouldn't. Vish liked to avoid the landlord as much as possible. Silas was strange and marginal. His apartment, in the back of the building on the ground floor beside the laundry room, always smelled like old fish and burnt cheese. He consistently shot down all Vish's tentative suggestions—that he buy a lock for the dumpster to deter the scavengers who crawled in there each week to look for salvage, that he clean and fill the pool, that he replace the broken locks on the mailboxes—and Vish always left their encounters feeling whiny and ineffectual.

Troy, on the other hand… No one could ever accuse Troy of being ineffectual. Troy was a cheerful force of nature. She rapped on Silas's door and introduced herself with a firm handshake and a knee-weakening smile, then took him by the hand and pulled him upstairs to examine the hole in the bathroom wall before he could think of some way to blow her off.

Silas flicked a soiled rag at the grubs to shoo them back into the hole, then nailed a square of plywood across the gap. He grunted.

"I'll patch it later," he said. "Get some plaster up over it, paint it, it'll be good as new." He straightened up and squinted at Vish. "Happened in the quake, you said?"

"It must have," Vish said. "I didn't notice it until today."

Silas made some noise in the back of his throat. "Sure you kids weren't messing around in here?"

"Digging a hole to China?" Vish asked. "No. It happened in the quake."

Silas shrugged. "Well, you'd say that, wouldn't you?"

"This is a great building," Troy said, her tone chipper. "These units are really roomy."

Silas looked at her, his scowl lightening. "They are, aren't they? Wouldn't know it from the outside exactly, but they're not bad."

"I saw the for-rent sign on the fence," Troy said. "Bad market right now, isn't it?"

"Goddamn economy," Silas said.

"If you cleaned and filled the pool, I bet the building would fill right up," she said. "You can see it from the sidewalk. It'd be a huge draw."

That seemed unlikely—pools were common in the neighborhood, and they certainly weren't a necessity this close to the beach—but when Troy said things, people listened. Silas started to look half-convinced, then he shook his head.

"No one'd use it," he said. "Summer's gone."

"Does it matter? You'd fill up the building. It'd pay for itself right there." Troy looked relaxed and engaged, like she was having a fantastic time chatting about pools with Silas, even though Silas was tedious and off-putting. This made Vish worry a bit, because she looked at him exactly the same way whenever they were alone together. Maybe she thought Vish was tedious and off-putting, too.

No. It'd be the easiest thing in the world for her to vanish out of his life if she didn't want to spend time with him, and yet here she was, dangling a promising job opportunity in front of him and cooking him a tasty meal. It had to mean something, something good.

CHAPTER EIGHT

VISH NEXT SAW Troy on Sunday at her tea party, which was held at her place in Hermosa Beach. Troy and her roommate shared the bottom level of a two-story condo. Their sliding patio doors opened directly onto the Strand, the snaking concrete path that ran along the coastline for much of the South Bay. Just beyond the path lay a satiny ribbon of sand and then the ocean, white-blue and boundless.

Apart from the view, Troy's place was a disappointment. An enormous flat-screen television taking up one corner of the living room, a white suede couch and matching armchair, a glass coffee table on a white wicker frame. White walls adorned with a framed *Breakfast At Tiffany's* poster, one that probably hung in the dorm rooms of cute young theater majors nationwide. No bookcases, no books. A short stack of *Interstellar Boys* scripts on the floor beside the sofa, a gossip magazine on the coffee table.

She shared the place with another woman. Maybe it was just the effect of having a roommate that made their communal living space so bland. Vish had shuffled through a succession of amiable-yet-distant roommates in his post-college years, and in each case their decor ended up with a similar generic quality. Something to do with compromise, not wishing to assert his own tastes too much, suppressing his personality for the sake of roommate bonhomie. Maybe Troy was the same.

Or maybe Troy just liked Audrey Hepburn and frothy magazines, and maybe she had better things to do with her time than decorate, and maybe he should stop being so damn judgmental.

Troy seemed delighted to see him. He'd worried about this a little. He was in his work garb, the black pants and the silly red vest that marked him as a member of the service industry, whereas she was the party's hostess and star attraction. Maybe the dichotomy would make her re-evaluate her interest in him. But she met him at the door with a hug and a quick kiss on his cheek, as though this was the most natural situation in the world. Today she smelled like tangerines.

"I was hoping it'd be you," she said. "I almost called your boss—Jamie, right?—to ask for you specifically, but I didn't want it to seem like I was *summoning* you."

"I'm glad you're okay about this. I was hoping you wouldn't find it weird," he said.

"Are you kidding? I'm thrilled," she said. She took him by the hand and led him over to the couch, where a gaunt, gangly young woman with straight black hair and an excess of dark eyeliner lounged against the cushions. "I want you to meet my roommate. Lola, this is Vish. You remember me telling you about him."

"Sure." Lola lifted a thin white arm in the air and languidly waved it, flashing chipped cobalt nails in his direction. "Hey."

"Nice to meet you," Vish said. Lola half-smiled, pale lips twitching. She gave him a slow once-over, head to toe, and seemed amused by whatever she saw.

"Likewise, I'm sure," she said. Her voice was a low drawl, her tone a whisper away from sarcasm. "Troy says you're going to serve us?"

"That's the idea, yes," Vish said.

"Fabulous." Lola's half-smile deepened into a smirk and she glanced over at Troy as though expecting her to share in some private joke, but Troy's attention was focused on Vish.

"Let me show you where to set up," Troy said. She led him over to the attached kitchen. "Stove, sink, refrigerator. Is there anything else you need?"

"I think I'm good. Thanks." Vish glanced in the fridge, which was shiny stainless steel, industrial and cavernous. It held half a head of cabbage, a lonely Styrofoam takeout container splattered with marinara, and twelve bottles of Cristal, chilling before the party.

Setting up was easy. No fussing with chafing dishes and butane burners, just a matter of arranging dainty cakes and pastries on decorative trays and brewing teas—rose Darjeeling and blackberry-ginger—in heavy silver urns. He'd transported the food and equipment in the company van, putting his long-neglected driver's license to use for once.

Guests arrived in twos and threes, maybe two dozen all total. All female, all sporting the glossy, well-groomed pretti-ness of working actresses, though for all Vish knew, they could be screenwriters, or mechanics, or gastroenterologists like Kate. Shiny hair, white teeth, flawless skin, slim figures.

Invisible in his service-industry trappings, Vish watched as they murmured over the trays of pastries, or perched on the sofa and sipped at flutes of champagne, or sat on the floor, long legs pulled close to their bodies. They ate very little and laughed a great deal.

After the last bottle of champagne had been poured out and Troy had shooed away the last guest amidst a flurry of giggles and hugs, he found himself alone with her. Lola had excused herself as well, leaving with one of the partygoers on a shopping excursion to nearby Santa Monica.

"Do you want to keep the leftovers?" he asked.

"Sure, why not? I can bring them to work tomorrow," Troy said. "It'll give us something to snack on during the read-through."

She stepped in to help with the cleanup, unasked. While Vish scrubbed out the silver urns in the sink, Troy loaded the tiny china plates and champagne flutes into the dishwasher. And when everything was clean and he was preparing to say his goodbyes, she placed a hand on either side of his face, stood on her toes, and kissed him.

It was strong, and vigorous, and surprisingly rough, like she was sucking all the breath, the strength, the life right out of him. Vish had an almost physical sensation of barriers falling down beneath the force of her kiss. After a moment of hesitation, he returned it.

So strange, this physical connection, this sensation of another body—a warm, firm body—against his, of another pair of arms sliding up and around him, of small hands gripping his shoulders and pulling him close. And then the arms were moving, sliding again, down his back and around his waist to the button of his cheap black slacks, and then one of those warm, nimble hands slipped inside his underwear and cupped him. He hardened at her touch.

Troy broke the kiss long enough to press her cheek against his. "The counter. Lift me up on the counter," she said, her words little more than a gasp. Small teeth nipped at his earlobe.

Vish moved his hands to her waist, so slender beneath her loose sweatshirt, then hesitated. "Wait. Are we going to…?"

Troy laughed, breathless and laced with irritation. "Why do you think I hustled everyone out of here?" she asked. "Lola knows. She'll be gone for hours. We've got the place to ourselves for as long as we want it." She slid a hand up his neck and fanned her fingers along his jawbone. "Don't try to tell me you don't want to."

"I do. I do." Vish swallowed hard. "But I wasn't planning… I don't have—"

"Bathroom," Troy said. "The one off of my bedroom, down the hall to the right. There's a box in the medicine cabinet." She winked and released him, then boosted herself up onto the kitchen counter. She crossed her legs, tanned and smooth under her white shorts. "I'll wait here for you."

"I'll be right back," Vish said. His pants were unbuttoned and on the verge of falling off his hips. He fastened them again, fingers thick and clumsy. He felt awkward and panicked, like he was on the verge of ruining an unreal, mind-crushingly great moment that would never come again.

He found Troy's bedroom. White walls, white dresser, white carpet. A framed poster of Van Gogh's *Irises* from LACMA hung above the bed, which was queen-sized and topped with a peach flowered coverlet and an assortment of ruffled pillows.

He checked his reflection in the bathroom mirror and winced. Hair plastered to his forehead with sweat, collar askew, one flap of his dumb vest tucked into his waistband. He straightened himself out as best he could, then went hunting in the medicine cabinet for Troy's stash of condoms.

Prescription bottles. Lots of them, a dozen or more, stored in an open plastic caddy in the medicine cabinet. The first medicine was for anxiety, the second for depression, and then he stopped reading the labels. This wasn't his business. It was a surprise that there were so many, but still, he had no right to snoop.

He found the condoms, extracted one from the box, and replaced the contents of the cabinet as best he could, feeling guilty.

Back to the kitchen, back to Troy, who was still perched on the counter, waiting for him. She smiled. "Found what you need?"

He held up the condom. "All good." He glanced around the kitchen, at the living room just beyond it, and beyond that the sliding doors and the Strand and all of Hermosa Beach. "Ah… we're kind of exposed here."

Troy shrugged. "We're not, not really. It's darker in here than it is outside. No one can see us unless they plaster their faces against the glass. It's fine."

"I suppose so." Vish looked outside again, uncertain. "We could always move to your bedroom."

"Or we could stay here." Troy's tone was light, but there was a trace of something beneath it. Impatience, or irritation. Fair enough. He was, in fact, dithering. She extended both arms toward him. "Don't ruin this."

He stepped forward and let his arms slide up around her ribcage, almost of their own accord. Her mouth closed on his once again.

Drowning in her, losing himself in the scent of tangerines, her heartbeat like the pounding of the ocean, her mouth sour with the taste of champagne. And when it was over, and they were sticky with sweat and bodily fluids, arm and thigh muscles twitching from their participation in this most ancient of sports, Troy wrapped her arms around his neck and pressed her forehead against his chest. "Let's walk on the beach," she said.

His time wasn't his own. He was on the clock, technically, and he still had to return to the shop and unload the equipment and help Jamie fix sandwiches and brew tea for customers. But it would be ungentlemanly to leave Troy now, so he nodded. "Sure."

They walked on the Strand, Troy's hand in his. The air was damp and the sky was whitish gray, the pale and feeble sun unable to burn away the marine layer. The South Bay was different than the beaches around Vish's apartment. Preppier than ratty Venice, less crowded than tourist-jammed Santa Monica. White-haired boys with shiny brown torsos played volleyball on the sand, wetsuited surfers paddled out into the waves, bronze-skinned girls in tiny bikinis reclined in folding beach chairs.

"You're quiet," Troy said at last. "Are you okay with this? Did I push you into this too quickly?"

He glanced down. She looked concerned, almost worried. "No, it's fantastic. Thank you very much. It just… I'm a little surprised, that's all."

Troy smiled. "I'm not usually like that," she said. "I mean, I'm always pretty forward, you know that about me, but I'm not usually that direct, if you know what I'm saying. But I really like being around you, Vish."

"I'm glad. Me too," Vish said. He took a deep breath. "I'd like to see more of you, Troy. A whole lot more."

It was hard to say. His stomach seemed to constrict, as though by exposing his neediness to Troy, he expected to be punched in the gut.

Laughter exploded out of her, a blast of unfettered amusement that instantly made him feel better. "I should hope so," she said. "I wouldn't have done that if I thought you didn't want this to be a regular thing. You and me, I mean." She gripped his hand tighter. "I'm not seeing anyone else right now. I want you to know that."

"Me either. I haven't seen anyone since moving to Los Angeles." He shrugged. "For a long time before that, actually."

She was quiet for a moment, her small features pensive. "Have you ever been in a serious relationship?" she asked.

Vish wanted to lie, because he didn't want her to think he was abnormal, but he wasn't sure how to be anything less than wholly honest with Troy. "Not really. I've dated before, but… No. Nothing anyone would consider serious. Nothing lasting."

She nodded, mulling this over. "Any particular reason why not?"

"People aren't drawn to me, I guess. The people I like never like me in return. Or if they do, they don't tell me about it."

"That might explain a few things," Troy said. "You never having a steady girlfriend, I mean."

"Oh?"

She shook her head. "The way you've been so ridiculously skittish about me thus far, I figured you either weren't interested, or you weren't sure how to proceed. Guess it's the second option." She turned to look at him. "I thought you'd call me, or email after we last met. We had a good time, a really good time, but you didn't follow up. If you didn't show up at my party today, I was going to give up on you."

"I'm sorry," he said. "I'm really sorry. I'm awkward with people a lot of the time, and I thought if I called, you'd think I was pushy or clingy, because…"

"Because?"

"Because I don't know what you're getting out of this relationship," Vish said. "You're beautiful and famous, and you're so nice to me it's almost unreal, and I don't know what you see in me. The whole thing seems, I don't know, weird."

He regretted the word "weird" as soon as it was out of his mouth. She stared at him for a moment, not amused. "Holy crap, Vish," she said at last. "Is that the way your brain works? I like you, and I want to spend time with you and help you out any way I can. Can't you accept that without thinking there's something funny going on?"

Her cheeks were flushed, her mouth was set in a grim line, and she was clearly pissed off. "I'm sorry," Vish said. "I didn't mean—"

"I like you," she said again. "That's all there is to it. Just relax and let this play out as it will, okay?"

She smiled her nice smile at him, and Vish felt a sense of relief at being forgiven so easily. "Okay," he said. "Sorry."

"Let's just walk," she said. She squinted up at the overcast sky. "Not that it's the best day for it."

They continued down the Strand until it ended near Redondo, then they walked on the sand until they reached the pier, which is where they first saw the surfers. Or at least Vish mentally categorized them as surfers, even though they weren't carrying boards or wearing wetsuits. They had on ratty Hawaiian shirts with wild flower prints, open to the waist and paired with baggy board shorts and battered sandals. They looked like surfers from a 1970s television show.

Correction: They looked like *villainous* surfers from a 1970s television show, the kind who'd antagonize the hero and make uncouth gestures toward the heroine. There were five of them, hanging out in a pack, passing around a hand-rolled cigarette. Longish tangled hair, shell necklaces against deeply tanned skin, their hairy legs and dirty feet incongruous amongst the white-bread affluence of the South Bay.

As Vish and Troy approached, their conversation stilled. Vish tried not to pay any attention to them, but he could feel hostile eyes on him.

A muttered statement: "Dead man walking."

Vish didn't turn to see which one had said it. Troy stopped and stared at them. Vish wanted to keep walking, but she squeezed his hand once and pulled him to a stop. "What did you say?" she asked. Her tone was curious, nothing more.

The one who appeared to be their leader smiled. He was good-looking, almost classically handsome, with thick dark hair that reached his collarbone and a strong, patrician nose. He took a long, slow drag on the cigarette, then cocked his head to the side and stared at Troy through the amber lenses of his wraparound sunglasses. "Ah, that's where you've been keeping yourself, huh? You pop up in the damnedest places."

Vish looked at Troy in surprise. She seemed unconcerned. "Did you say something to my friend?"

The leader tossed his cigarette butt down and ground it out under the heel of his sandal. "I said he's a dead man walking."

"As threats go, that's not very good, is it?" Troy asked. She sounded as unflappable and friendly as ever. Vish thought he should jump in at some point, or lead Troy away from there, but he couldn't find any easy way to enter the conversation, and besides, she looked like she wouldn't appreciate his assistance. "I mean, that applies to everyone, doesn't it?"

The surfer smiled. "You do have a point there, friend." He gestured with his chin at Vish. "His day's coming quicker than most, though. Bad hoodoo surrounding that one. Not that you'd know anything about it."

Troy smiled, and for once it didn't look either friendly or pleasant. "Nice chatting with you boys," she said. She gripped Vish's hand tighter. "Let's go, Vish."

Vish let Troy lead him away from the group. "See you soon, Vish," the surfer called after him.

Vish's face felt hot. "What was that all about?" he asked Troy as soon as they were out of earshot. "Friends of yours?"

She shook her head. "No idea. I've never seen them before. Just a bunch of stoners, I guess." She smiled. It still looked a little tight. "Do kids say 'stoners' these days? I'm not up on my drug lingo."

"That one guy acted like he knew you. He said you pop up in the damnedest places," he said.

She rolled her eyes. "Maybe he's a huge *Interstellar Boys* fan. I don't really know." She looked at him. "I'm sorry if they weirded you out, but they were just a bunch of drugged-up assholes saying shit that probably makes sense when you're high. Anybody who happened to walk past them would've gotten the same treatment. It doesn't have anything to do with me, or with you." It was a little snappish.

"I'm sorry," Vish said. "I didn't mean to grill you."

"You weren't. Don't worry about it." She snorted. "They were kind of creepy, weren't they?"

It was good to hear her admit it, because something about the surfers had unsettled him. "Should we turn around? I have to get back to the shop soon," he said.

"Sure." Troy smiled, carefree and natural. She leaned up and kissed his cheek, and everything was okay again.

They walked back to Troy's place along the edge of the water. Troy dangled her sandals from one hand and padded barefoot on packed sand, letting the incoming waves splash over her feet. They detoured around kelp patches and the abandoned ruins of sand castles. Vish resisted the urge to glance back at the pier, where the surfers might still be lurking.

Troy helped him carry his supplies to the van and kissed him again before he climbed behind the wheel. "So..." Vish said.

"So Freddie still wants to talk to you about the show, but last week got crazy for us, and he didn't have time to get in touch with you. This week, for sure," Troy said. "I'll call when I know more and let you know what's up."

"Thank you," Vish said. "Thank you so much."

"I'll call," Troy said again. She stepped back and waved from the curb. He backed out of the parking space, then headed up to Sepulveda, back toward Venice, away from Troy and the surfers.

CHAPTER NINE

FREDDIE HALTERMAN, THE lauded creator of *Interstellar Boys*, was in his late thirties, early forties maybe. He was quiet and contained, almost bashful. He wore a striped button-down shirt over stiff, dark jeans that somehow looked wrong on him: too new, maybe, or too high at the waist, or maybe Freddie just felt uncomfortable and unnatural in them, the way Vish felt whenever he wore a suit. Which is what he was wearing today, because this was a job interview, or something like it, and he wanted to look professional.

Freddie had a receding chin and a thick mustache that swamped his upper lip. When he smiled at Vish, the mustache moved up to smother his nostrils in brown fuzz.

"Troy really talked you up and down, and I have to say, I think she picked a winner." He pawed through a mess of loose papers on his desk, picked up a script, squinted at it, tossed it aside. "I thought I had your book here..."

There was nothing on his desk that could possibly be his book, which ran to about six hundred pages. Vish waited, smiling politely.

Freddie gave up the search with a shrug. He smiled at Vish again. "I thought it was really, really neat. Really... thick. So I guess you're from India, huh?"

"Born in Detroit," Vish said. "I've actually never been to India."

"That explains why you don't have an accent." Another smile, somewhat nervous. "You're a good writer. You don't have any television experience?"

"No. I just moved here at the start of the year. From New York. I've been trying to get a foothold into the industry, but I haven't had much luck."

"We can set you up on a trial basis." Freddie folded his hands together on top of one of the piles of paper. "We could use another staff writer. I don't think it'd take you long to get the hang of our format. Are you familiar with *Interstellar Boys*?"

"Yes, I am. I think it's an amazing show," Vish said. This was only half a lie. He'd watched the entire series over the past week, streaming it online on his laptop in preparation for this meeting. They were currently in the middle of the third season, and the first season, if not quite amazing, had been fun and trashy in a cheerful and mostly inoffensive way. Troy was great in it, even though her role as a spaceship commander-slash-astrophysicist wasn't a meaty one. She was sexy yet practical, managing to seem plausibly brainy even while scampering about a spaceship in silver hotpants and matching knee-high boots. The show was undeniably cheesy, but it was knowing, deliberate cheese with some wit behind it.

In the second and third seasons, though, it had derailed. Vish continued watching with a sinking sensation as interesting characters stagnated or vanished, as promising plotlines were abandoned or burdened with nonsensical complications. He'd slogged his way through the most recent episodes, because of course he'd need to be familiar with those, but it had been a struggle.

Season Two was when the bumblebee girl joined the cast. Kelsey Kirkpatrick, the girl who'd teetered on the patio railing at that party in the hills the night of the earthquake. She'd come on the show, bringing her cachet as the star of a number of tween-oriented films, playing a nubile young stowaway with psychic powers, and as soon as she appeared, the focus shifted further away from Troy.

Still, though, he could write for it, warts and all. Maybe he'd have some positive effect. He could provide a fresh outside perspective. He'd already scribbled down a handful of ideas to help nudge the characters back in the direction of the roles that had been originally established for them.

"Well, then." Freddie smiled at him. "I'm excited about this. Start on Monday?"

A quick pang of guilt. Jamie had always been good to him, signing him up for extra hours whenever he needed them; he should return the favor by giving her more than a couple days' notice. "Absolutely."

Freddie rose to his feet and extended a hand. Vish shook it. "Welcome to *Interstellar Boys*, Vish. Good to have you with us."

When Vish emerged from Freddie's office, Troy was waiting for him in the reception area. She sat cross-legged in an overstuffed chair, leafing through her script, oblivious to the gigantic framed promotional poster of herself looming above her head. She looked up, her face expectant. "Well?"

"He hired me," Vish said. He sounded dazed.

79

"Fantastic!" Troy unfolded herself from the chair and stood up. She hugged him and gave him a peck on the chin. "I knew he would. I didn't want to tip my hand too much, but I knew Freddie wanted you. Congratulations."

"It's all thanks to you. I wouldn't have been able to get in the door without your help," he said.

Troy waved this aside. "You got this on your own. You're an amazing writer. We could really use you right now." She had never spoken about *Interstellar Boys* with anything other than high praise, bordering on hyperbole. This was the closest she'd come to acknowledging the current troubles.

She took his hand. "Come on. I want you to meet everyone."

The production offices and the stages were located in the same facility on the dingy southeast end of Hollywood. Troy had been due on set at six that morning, so Vish had shown up for his afternoon meeting with Freddie by himself, surprising the guard at the gate by approaching on foot instead of driving.

He and Troy crossed through the studio lot, which was vast and empty and silent. Vish had a mental image of what it should look like: costumers wheeling racks of clothes to and from trailers, stagehands hauling gigantic props and backdrops, construction workers hammering away at sets, production assistants fetching coffee for their high-powered bosses. This, however, was a ghost town.

"What else films here?" he asked. "Other television shows?"

Troy shrugged. "Back in our first season, there were three or four other series shooting here. Right now, there's not much. Sometimes they do infomercials, stuff like that. I talked to a girl last week who was taping a pilot on the stage next to ours." She glanced around the silent lot and frowned. "It comes in waves, I guess."

She led him through the side door of a monstrous white windowless building with "STAGE 3" painted on the side in story-high block letters. Inside it was dark and cavernous. In the center of the room, plywood backdrops surrounded three sides of a set. It was the bridge of the starship, where most of the action on *Interstellar Boys* took place. On television, it looked sleek and airy and ethereal, with pale backlit monitors and sculpted chrome chairs and frosted translucent walls. Up close, vacant and unlit, it looked flimsy and silly, just painted plywood and acrylic sheeting.

Large men in work shirts and jeans bustled around the studio, coiling cables and setting up lights. "What's happening today?" Vish asked Troy. He kept his voice hushed, even though it was obvious no cameras were rolling. "Are you going to be filming?"

Troy shook her head. "We did some location shooting in Riverside this morning, and now they're setting up for the shoot later this afternoon, but I'm done for the day." She wore street clothes, a long sweater over leggings, but there were dark smears in the corners of her eyes, lingering traces of the heavy makeup she wore while filming. She glanced around. "I don't see anyone. Let's try Ridpath's trailer first."

That must be Ridpath Washburn, who played the ship's engineer, Dudge. Vish had boned up on the cast members and production staff before his meeting. He followed Troy outside and around to the back of the stage, where a half-dozen trailers were parked in two parallel rows. Troy climbed up the lightweight metal steps of the nearest trailer and rapped her knuckles on the screen door. "Hey, Ridpath? You in there?"

The door flew open. Ridpath, bare-chested and in track pants, ran a hand over his shaved head and squinted at her. "What's up, doll?"

"Got someone I want you to meet." She beckoned for Vish to step forward. "This is my friend Vish. Freddie just hired him as a writer. Vish, this is Ridpath."

"Hey, man." Ridpath held the door open and stood to the side. "Come in, y'all. I was just lying down, so it's kind of messy in here."

Ridpath's trailer was small and comfortable, with a kitchenette on one side and a built-in sofa running the length of the other. Ridpath scooped up a fleece blanket and a couple of throw pillows and stuffed them into a mesh overhead bin, then gestured at the sofa. "Have a seat. Can I get you anything to drink… was your name Fish? Did I hear that right?"

"Vish. With a V."

"Vish, sorry. Cool name. I'm going to make myself some coffee, want any? I've got bottled water, too."

"Coffee would be great. Thank you."

Ridpath ran water into an electric kettle and plugged it in, then measured grounds into a French press. His movements were precise and contained. He looked burly and bulky on

82

television, with a thick neck and a powerful upper body, but in the flesh, he was surprisingly compact. He was an inch or so taller than Vish, which put him just under six feet, and his shoulders, while sculpted with well-defined musculature, were narrow. Petite, even.

"Is Kelsey still around?" Troy asked.

Ridpath shook his head. "I don't know, doll. She left to tape an interview a while ago. I haven't seen her come back."

"I'm going to see if she's here. I want her to meet Vish, too," Troy said. She patted Vish on the wrist. "Keep Ridpath entertained, okay? You boys can swap gossip about me. I'll be back in a minute."

She gave Vish a kiss on the cheek, fast and affectionate, then left. Ridpath sat on the narrow couch beside Vish while waiting for the kettle to boil. "So you're writing for us, huh?"

"So it seems. I just got the offer a few minutes ago, so it doesn't quite seem real yet. I'm looking forward to it, though. The show's great."

"Yeah. Sure is." Was Vish hearing things, or was there an undercurrent of sarcasm there? "So. You and my girl Troy are friends, huh?" Ridpath leaned over and ran a brown thumb lightly over Vish's cheek where Troy had kissed him. "Good friends?"

Vish could feel himself blushing. "Yeah. Pretty good." He'd better follow Troy's lead on this. Maybe she wouldn't want her costars and coworkers to know she'd snagged her under-credited and under-qualified new boyfriend a job as a writer.

Ridpath smiled. It was a nice smile, full of charm. He had very straight, very thick eyebrows and a strong, magnificent nose. "How long have you known her?" he asked.

"Just a couple weeks," Vish said. It seemed ridiculous that so much could change in such a short time. "I met her the day after that earthquake."

"She's happy about you," Ridpath said. He shrugged. "I'm assuming it's you, at least. She's been a different person over the past week or so. Much less neurotic. I mean, I love Troy, we all do, but most of the time, girlfriend needs to chill. Lately, though? She's been a dream on set. If that's thanks to you, we owe you one."

Vish blinked. Troy was about the least neurotic person he'd ever met.

"Were you the one to get her to quit smoking?" Ridpath asked. He shook his head. "Cold turkey, man. That couldn't have been easy."

The kettle boiled; Ridpath got to his feet and dumped steaming water over the coffee grounds. Vish stared at his back.

"Troy doesn't smoke," he said. He frowned. "Does she?"

"Up until last week, she sure as hell did. After every single take, she'd scurry outside to light up, which kind of sucked for those of us who just wanted to finish our damn scene. Freddie sat her down last season and had a talk with her about it, and she ripped him a new one. " Ridpath shrugged. "And then last week, she stopped. No fuss, no drama. Didn't even mention it until I asked her what was up, and then she just said something about how it was time to clean up some bad habits."

"I can't take credit for that," Vish said. "I've never seen her smoke before. I had no idea." Huh. Maybe the interior of Troy's car had smelled a bit like stale tobacco on the day they first met, now that he thought back on it.

Ridpath depressed the plunger on the French press in one slow, steady motion. "Maybe she did it on the sly because she thought you wouldn't want to date a smoker. People do incredible things when they're in love."

Love. Maybe Ridpath was exaggerating, but Vish still felt a small tingle in his spine at the word and all it contained.

The trailer door burst open, and Troy came in, pulling Kelsey Kirkpatrick, minus the bumblebee dress, behind her. In an oversized t-shirt over sweatpants, Kelsey seemed an even more unlikely object of adult lust than she had at Maryanne's party. With her crop of lemon-colored hair and her round cherub face, she looked tiny and fresh-scrubbed.

"Vish, this is Kelsey. Kels, meet Vish. He's the one I've been telling you about."

Kelsey gave Vish a friendly wave. "He's cute," she said to Troy. There was a faint note of surprise in her tone. She turned to Vish. "You're so not like the guys Troy usually dates. And that's a really good thing."

"Kelsey..." Troy rolled her eyes.

"Seriously. She's gone through this whole string of beefheads. They all blend together in my brain."

Troy's cheeks went pink. "I think that's probably all Vish wants to hear about that particular subject," she said.

"You're bringing him to my birthday party, aren't you?" Kelsey asked.

Troy frowned. "That's, what, next month?"

"Yeah. The seventeenth. But I need to have the guest list in stone, so let me know for sure if you're coming. The restaurant's kind of small."

Kelsey's eighteenth birthday. Wasn't that what Toby had been yammering about in a mildly salacious way at Maryanne's party? A dark thought crept in, unwanted and unwarranted: Would he and Troy even still be together in a month, given the speed at which their relationship had developed?

In any case, they'd both be working on the show. They'd be spending lots of time together, one way or another. As Ridpath poured coffee for everyone, Troy caught Vish's eye and winked. It was a wink filled with affection and promise, and it helped quiet the nagging doubts.

CHAPTER TEN

JAMIE TOOK HIS resignation well, though she was clearly disappointed. "*Interstellar Boys*?" she said. "Wow. That's really cool, Vish. Congratulations." She paused. "Did you know Troy Van Ellen before this? Is that why she hired us to cater her party?"

"No. I met her for the first time when she stopped by the shop." Vish thought for a moment, then gave Jamie a stripped-down version of events. "We ended up talking about my writing career, and she passed along my book to the executive producer, who hired me."

"Well, fantastic. I'm glad that worked out so well for you," she said. "We're going to miss you, though. Especially since we're getting into the holiday season."

"I know. I'm sorry."

She waved a hand. "It's a great opportunity. Don't feel guilty." She smiled. "I'm sure you'll be great and they'll love you, but if things don't work out on the show, you and your napkin-folding skills are welcome back any time."

"Thanks, Jamie." It was weird. Vish had been ambivalent about the catering job from the start; Jamie had been a stellar boss, but he'd come to Los Angeles to write. This was his first opportunity to get paid for doing just that. So why did he feel like giving notice to Jamie was a mistake?

Because things had happened with alarming speed, and because he was resistant to change, and because he was, at times, a fussbudget who tended to get in his own way. Writing for *Interstellar Boys* was nothing but a good thing, any way he looked at it.

He only had to work with the other writers. Nobody said he had to like them.

Vish included, there were twelve. Most were also credited as producers, or consulting producers, or supervising producers, or executive producers. They all huddled in a big conference room around a long table littered with pizza boxes and water bottles. A whiteboard on the far wall was covered with scribbled notations on a crudely-drawn grid. The ink from the markers had dissolved over time, leaving illegible fragments of words. It was a breakdown of episodes long past and long forgotten; Vish had spent much of the past hour examining the board, and he had yet to see anything on there apropos to the current season.

A couple of the writers looked like they could still be in college. They were all young, twenties or early thirties, with the exception of Freddie, who sat at the head of the table. All were male, and Vish was far and away the darkest person in the room.

"Oh, right," one of the writers said when Freddie first introduced him to the group. "You're from the diversity program, right? Cool deal."

"I'm sorry?"

The writer shrugged. Ken, Vish later learned his name was. He wore a t-shirt and shorts, and he liked leaning back in his chair, hands behind his neck, and propping his dirty flip-flops up on the table, smack next to the pizzas. "There's some kind of big charity program where they stick minorities on writing staffs. Is that where you came from?"

"Ah… no," Vish said.

"Vish is a friend of Troy's," Freddie said, his tone mild.

Ken shrugged. "Sorry, dude," he said. "Just as well. Everyone they've sent us from there has sucked. If you're black or a girl, it's eighty times easier to get a job writing for television than if you're a white guy. Seriously."

Seriously? Vish looked around the table at all the white male faces and remained silent.

"Oh, that one chick we had. What was her name? She was the worst." That came from Bob. It was a toss-up as to whether Vish despised Ken or Bob more. It pretty much depended upon which was speaking at any given time.

"She wasn't from the program," Ken said. "I don't know where they found her. Probably sucked off some bigwig at the network, because she sure as hell couldn't write." He shrugged. "She used to bitch us out about how our show was sexist. I mean, we've got a lady character who's both a god-damned astrophysicist and a black belt. That sounds pretty progressive to me, right?"

Vish said nothing, maintaining an indeterminate half-smile, hoping this was some weird freshman-writer hazing ritual.

The day went downhill from there. Vish wasn't expected to participate yet—Freddie advised him just to observe at first—but this was a situation that could go nowhere good. After a morning spent gamely following along, his brain shut down in protest, tuning out the overlapping chatter of the writers as they bounced around ideas. The ideas came in waves of incoherence, each more preposterous and salacious than the last.

"I think we need a big arc for Starla," Freddie said. "Something that'll really show her chops. She's been back-burnered for too much of the season."

Vish perked up. Commander Starla was Troy's character, the astrophysicist with the black belt, and Freddie's observation was the only statement in the meeting thus far with which he wholeheartedly agreed.

"I think she should get raped," Ken said. "That would give her something really dramatic, huh? People would be talking about it."

"Dudge could do it," Bob said. "We set up some sparks between Dudge and Starla way back, didn't we? So that would take their relationship to another stage."

Vish sat up in his chair. He cleared his throat. "Does that make sense, though?" he asked. Everyone turned to look at him. "Dudge is one of the good guys. We haven't seen him do anything thus far that would suggest he'd turn into rapist."

"Even good guys snap," Ken said. "That's why this would be a cool storyline. We'd show how the stress of being in space for so long is really getting to them. Dudge falls madly in love with Starla and then goes too far, and she feels betrayed and uncertain." He kept going, his voice growing louder, building on his theme. "But she doesn't tell anyone about it because she's ashamed, and meanwhile Dudge keeps stalking her around the ship. Leaving her roses on her pillow, shit like that."

"If you make him a rapist, the audience will turn against his character forever," Vish said. He tried to keep his tone as neutral as possible.

"Not if we handle it correctly," Freddie said. "Some of the most nuanced characters in television history have been villains. We'd be giving him layers. Done right, it's good character development. And I think there's a tendency among viewers to see Starla as too ball-busting and competent, so this could show them her human side."

Vish glanced around the room at the rest of the writing staff. A few looked interested in the conversation, a few others typed away on their laptops or tablets. Maybe they were taking notes or jotting down ideas. Maybe they were checking email, or surfing porn. Maybe he should start bringing his laptop to work.

"Ken, why don't you and Bob have a powwow this afternoon and pound out the details? Email me your treatment for the storyline by the end of the day, and then you can start on the script." Freddie continued around the table, assigning bits and pieces of multiple storylines to individual writers. This, Vish had gleaned, was his usual method. At the end of the week, the episode would be then cobbled together, piecemeal-style.

Vish did not receive an assignment, nor did at least half of the other writers. What were they expected to do for the rest of the day? Maybe his entire position on the staff would consist of this, sitting in on endless meetings and eating free pizza.

The meeting broke up. He headed to his newly-assigned cubicle, which was bare except for a computer and a stack of health-plan brochures given to him at the new-employee orientation he'd attended that morning. The sight cheered him up. He'd receive a hefty paycheck each week until the show went on summer hiatus in March (unless he was canned before that, a little voice inside his head reminded him). This was a job many would envy, perfect for putting some flesh on his malnourished résumé.

He looked over at Mark, the writer occupying the cubicle next to him. Mark hadn't spoken much during the meeting; when Vish, his attention drifting, had happened to meet his glance, he'd rolled his eyes in what seemed like commiseration.

Mark smiled at him. "Enjoy your first creative meeting?"

"Very much," Vish said. "It was interesting." He paused. "Ah… what should I be doing now?"

Mark shrugged. He had curly hair, already receding though he was probably younger than Vish, and wire-rimmed glasses. "Check email. Hang out in the break room and watch TV. Doesn't really matter. I was going to head over to the set for a bit. Want to come with?"

"Sure. Thanks." He followed Mark across the empty lot to the big white soundstage.

They were quiet. Finally, Mark spoke. "So. What'd you think?"

Vish considered. "I think I'm a little unclear as to what I should be doing here," he said cautiously.

"Collecting a paycheck," Mark said. "As near as I can tell, that's what I was hired to do." He smiled at Vish. "Attend the meetings. Participate in the brainstorming and bring up your story ideas, by all means, but don't expect them to go anywhere. Work on the script whenever Freddie tells you to write something. If you're one of his pets, that will be daily. If you're like me, that won't be often." He gave Vish a sidelong glance. "Don't take this the wrong way, but at a guess, you're not going to be one of his pets."

"Ah," Vish said. "And Ken would be?"

"Ken and Bob, mainly. A few of the others, too. Sure. Ken and Bob were Freddie's assistants on the first season, before they got promoted. They're simpatico with him." Mark shrugged. "It's how Freddie wants to run things, and he's the boss. Hard to get work these days, especially in entertainment, and I'm getting paid a lot of money to sit in on some meetings. Not a bad deal, really."

No, it wasn't, not when it was laid out like that. Vish felt better. There'd been something hostile and acrid in the meeting room, but now that feeling was dissipating in the balmy air. The lot was studded with neat rows of palm trees, spindly stalks that rose up above the stages until they exploded like fireworks into mad bursts of spiky fronds. An iconic symbol of Los Angeles, all promise and potential and fresh starts.

A red light flashed above the closed door to the sound-stage. Mark and Vish waited until it went out, signifying a break in filming, then slipped inside.

The main set, the spaceship bridge, was drenched in bright studio lights. Costumed actors huddled in consultation with the episode's director, a gaunt man in a baseball cap and jeans. Vish looked around, but didn't see Troy.

Mark gestured with his head to the end of the stage where the craft services table was set up. Great platters of sandwiches with cold cuts and cheese spilling out of crusty Kaiser rolls. An assortment of salads: something with feta and multicolored olives, cold tortellini with pesto and crabmeat, chunks of fresh fruit and berries. Coffee, sodas, baskets of Frisbee-sized cookies and brownies.

Mark picked up a plate and began grazing. Vish had filled up on pizza in the writers' room. Too bad. He'd have to remember to save room next time. He looked up and saw Freddie heading over to them.

"Hey, Mark. Vish." Freddie nodded at them both. "How's it going here?"

"Really well, Freddie. Scene looks great," Mark said. Mark must be precognitive, since the cameras hadn't rolled since they'd entered the stage.

"What'd you think of the meeting?" Freddie asked Vish.

"Very interesting. I enjoyed it," Vish said. "It was my first experience with anything like that. They seem like a good group." He sounded chipper. Good.

"They are, they really are. Smart bunch of guys. Some of the best writers in the business," Freddie said. He paused.

"One thing that I really try my best to reiterate, everyone needs to feel totally comfortable expressing an opinion. Even if it's not necessarily the most diplomatic, or the most 'correct'"—and here, Freddie used finger quotes to make his point—"it's all part of the creative process, and it's all valuable to us. Right?"

"Sure," Vish said. "Of course. I get that."

"Good. Good." Freddie cleared his throat. "You didn't sound too enthusiastic about the idea for Dudge's plotline."

"I'd have to see how it was executed," Vish said. He picked his next words with care. "From my viewpoint, it seems as though it might be a mistake to turn a regular character—a character who's been pretty sympathetic thus far—into a rapist. Just speaking as a fan, I don't think I've seen any indication that this would be a logical path for Dudge."

"But it's like I said. Characters change and grow, sometimes in ways the audience doesn't necessarily approve of. I think if you'd learn to open your mind a little more, you'd see how this could really be an interesting development for Dudge and Troy—and for the show. Okay?"

"Sure. No problem."

"Good." Freddie gave him another smile and a quick pat on the arm, then shuffled over toward the action on the set.

Vish exhaled, short and violent. He turned to Mark. "Was I out of line in the meeting?"

"By objecting to having Dudge rape Starla?" Mark rolled his eyes. "I wish I could tell you that was the most objectionable idea that's been raised in that room."

Mark picked his way through the salads on his plate with his fingers and popped a purple olive into his mouth. "My advice? Don't waste energy arguing. If Freddie thinks something's a good idea, it's going to make its way into the script."

Vish nodded, digesting this. He wished he had the sort of personality that could enable him to take charge of meetings, to suggest powerful and evocative plotlines that would win back viewer acclaim and reverse the downward trajectory the show had been on for the past two seasons, but that wasn't in his nature. Which was probably why he had no money, no car, and no noteworthy accomplishments to his name.

He did have a smoking-hot TV-star girlfriend, though. When Mark wandered off to talk to one of the production assistants, Vish looked around again for Troy. She was listed on the call sheet for this afternoon, which meant she was probably resting in her trailer. He could go looking for her, but she might prefer some time to herself to prepare for her scenes.

An actress approached the craft services table. A day player, not a series regular. She was in costume, a skimpy toga-style dress in sparkly lavender taffeta. Her dark hair was arranged in an elaborate topknot of coiled braids. She had a snub nose and a prominent overbite, and while she was maybe shy of being a knockout, she looked lively and pretty. She looked up from the table and grinned at Vish.

"God, those brownies look fabulous," she said. "I keep gravitating over here, even though I know I can't eat anything. With this costume, I've been sucking in my gut all morning as it is." She looked at Vish in curiosity. "What do you do on the show?"

"I'm one of the writers," he said. Maybe he should add a disclaimer after that, mention that he was on a trial basis, because he didn't belong on that staff yet. Maybe he never would. "I'm Vish."

"Carlotta," she said. They shook hands. "I'm playing Vera." At his blank look, she elaborated. "The tavern girl who gets mauled to death by the mysterious space entity?"

"Ah. I haven't seen the script for this episode." Which, if he thought about it, was kind of a strange thing for one of the writers to admit.

"It's a tiny part. I'm just here today and tomorrow," she said. "I always wanted to be a writer. You guys get a lot more respect than actors do."

"I'm not sure how true that is," Vish said. "I'm pretty sure I'm standing on the lowest rung of the ladder. I just started on the show today."

"Oh, wow." Carlotta looked around. "Do you feel any-where near as overwhelmed as I do?"

"Very likely, yes," Vish said. "Until last weekend, I was working as a caterer."

"I'm a waitress," Carlotta said. "At a Denny's in Pacoima, no kidding. This is my first paid acting job in like forever." She looked around the stage, then back at Vish. "Hey, I don't know how long I'm going to be here, but if we finish up around the same time, do you want to grab a drink later?"

"He's got plans." Vish jumped as Troy's arm slid around his waist. She was in her costume and heavy makeup, all long legs and stretchy silver fabric. She smiled at Carlotta and stuck out her hand. "Hi, I'm Troy. You're in the next scene with me, right?"

"Oh. I didn't…" Carlotta looked stricken, clearly afraid she'd made a career-derailing gaffe by flirting with the boyfriend of a cast member. She recovered and shook Troy's hand. "Really great to meet you, Troy. I'm Carlotta. I didn't know you and Vish…" She reddened.

Troy laughed. "Don't worry about it." Her dimples flashed. "Vish and I were just going to grab dinner nearby, if we get done here at a reasonable hour. We'd love to have you join us."

"I…" Carlotta looked wary, then relaxed. "Really? That would be great. If you don't mind."

"Perfect." Troy released Vish and linked her arm with Carlotta's. "One of the PAs told me they're about ready for us. Shall we?" With a wink and a wave at Vish, she led Carlotta over to the set, where the director and Freddie huddled in conversation.

There was something so *nice* about Troy. She didn't make a stink about little inconveniences, she was free of neuroses, she went out of her way to make everyone feel relaxed and welcome. Though from Ridpath's account, that wasn't always the case…

Vish stared after Troy and wondered.

CHAPTER ELEVEN

"It went well, I thought," Troy said. She settled back into her chair and glanced at Carlotta over the rim of her margarita. "Carlotta, you were great."

"Thanks. So were you. It was a fun day."

The three nestled into a corner table at a trendy Mexican bar down the street from the production facility. Carlotta had the only chair; Vish and Troy shared an upholstered bench that ran along the wall beneath a stylized mosaic of the Virgin Mary done in shiny bottle caps. A basket of multicolored tortilla chips and chunky guacamole sat on the table in front of them, but no one had touched it, Troy and Carlotta because working actresses didn't eat, and Vish because he'd grazed his way across the craft services table during the tedious evening of taping.

It was nice to unwind now with light conversation and margaritas that came in glasses the size of a human skull. Vish hadn't thought the day was fun. He'd thought it had been murderously long. But Troy appeared to think things were great, and whether her enthusiasm was real or feigned, it was infectious. Troy held her glass in one hand and kept her free hand on the small of his back. Vish could feel the angsty coil of stress in his spine unwind at her touch, and his dour mood lightened.

"How long have you two been together?" Carlotta asked. "You're a couple, right?"

"We are," Troy said. She broke into a huge smile, and Vish felt giddy. "It's been fast. We only met a couple weeks ago, but..." She widened her eyes. "It was obvious from the start that Vish and I had so much in common."

She told the story of their relationship from her perspective, about seeing Vish at the shop and realizing he was injured and marching him straight to the hospital. Maybe there was some Nightingale syndrome at work—maybe Troy had fallen for him because she could fuss over him and fix his life—but she certainly seemed to feel genuine affection toward him. Love, even. Maybe.

"That's so sweet," Carlotta said. "You two look great together." Her expression was wistful as she looked at them, and Vish understood that. He understood being alone and feeling purposeless and adrift. And now, with Troy, that was all behind him, and all he could do was smile at Carlotta in sympathy and hope things worked out for her.

Carlotta didn't show up on set the next day, which was odd. She'd seemed thrilled about the role; she'd left the restaurant sober and at a reasonable hour. Hard to imagine why she'd blown off the shoot.

When Freddie's office tried to reach her, she didn't answer her phone. One of the PAs drove out to her apartment in the Valley and pounded on her door, to no avail. Eventually, the scene she'd done with Troy was hastily re-shot with a replacement, summoned via a casting agent at the last second.

100

In the end, though, it hardly mattered, because the show went on an unexpected hiatus at the end of the week, with filming on the current episode unfinished.

In this case, "hiatus" was almost certainly a polite way of saying "canceled." The word was never spoken outright, but everyone knew the network was unhappy with the soggy ratings and thus had ordered production to cease for a month while the scripts for upcoming episodes were retooled and revised. After that, the network would make a decision as to whether to finish out the season, or cut their losses and scrap it.

Vish thought this meant he'd be called upon to work with the other writers during the hiatus. Freddie soon disabused him of this notion.

"It's just going to be me, and Bob, and Ken," Freddie said. "I think we'll be able to work more efficiently. The network says the recent episodes have seemed inconsistent. I don't really think that's the problem, I think viewers just weren't prepared to evolve with the show as it developed. Still..." He shrugged. "We've brought in too many new hires lately, and that's probably why some people think we've drifted off course. Things will be more cohesive if the writing is only handled by the core group."

This was announced during Friday's meeting in the writers room. It was Vish's fifth such meeting and, as seemed likely, his final one. His career as a television writer had lasted one business week.

Troy took the news well when Vish went to check on her in her trailer. "We'll be back," she said. "It's just a month. I know the ratings have dipped, but we still have a lot of supporters." She leaned forward in her chair and squinted at her reflection in the mirror. She was already out of her wardrobe and in her street clothes; her face was bare of makeup and shiny with moisturizer. "And if it doesn't come back, then it wasn't meant to be. Something better will come along for us."

Her eyes met his in the mirror. "I'm mostly just sorry for you. You barely had a chance to get started here."

"It's okay." It was. It totally was. He felt bad for Troy, who had far more emotional investment in the show than he did, but for his part, it was a bit of a relief.

"Ridpath is throwing a barbecue at his house tomorrow to... well, I guess 'celebrate' isn't the right term, is it?" Troy laughed. "I told him I'd check with you if we want to go."

"That sounds like fun. Sure."

"I'll let him know we'll be there," Troy said. "You sure you're okay with everything? You look a little... off or something."

"I'm fine. Maybe a little tired. It's an odd end to an odd week."

"I'm sure you're disappointed by all this. You've got to be."

"I don't think I am. Not yet, at least. Probably I will be once the news sinks in, but I don't know if I was a good fit with the other writers anyway."

"What do you mean?" Troy asked. "Because you didn't like their ideas?"

He shrugged. "Yeah. I guess."

"Ever consider that it might be your problem, too?" she asked. She turned in her chair to look at him. "I hear some people get good results from actually, like, going after things they want instead of waiting for stuff to magically happen to them."

There was an edge to it. "Are you mad at me?" he asked.

"No, of course not. But you're so damn passive sometimes. It'd be nice to see you get passionate and really go after something for once."

It stung, probably because it was true. "I'm sorry," he said.

Troy laughed. "And that's the perfect passive response." She waved a hand, dismissing the topic. "Sorry. I'm a little cranky about Freddie's announcement, and I'm picking a fight. Forgive me?"

"Always," Vish said.

Troy pulled him down onto the chair beside her, scooting over to give him room, and slipped her arm around his waist. He leaned against her and rested his head on her shoulder. In the mirror, they looked like a cute couple—clean-cut, attractive, affectionate with each other. For the first time, it felt like they matched.

So now Vish was unemployed. Easy come, easy go. He was in limbo since the show hadn't been formally canceled and he was still drawing a paycheck, but as soon as it was official, he'd go back and work for Jamie. Wouldn't be the worst thing in the world.

Troy moved in with him in an informal kind of way. She spent all her time at his apartment, which made a certain amount of sense. Since she had a roommate, it'd be inconvenient for him to stay at her place, and besides, he still didn't have a car. Much easier for Troy to zip up to Venice in her cute little two-seater than for him to trek down to Hermosa on the bus.

They had a good time together. They went to Ridpath's barbecue, held in the immaculate green backyard of the house he shared in Tarzana with Brad, his impossibly preppy boyfriend. They splashed around in the courtyard pool, which Silas had finally cleaned and filled, even though the days were growing colder. They received, via courier, a big lavender envelope stuffed with a ribbon-festooned invitation to Kelsey's birthday party.

They strolled through the grid of the Venice canals, with the rows of pretty houses lining both sides of the water and the tall palms swaying overhead. Nice, though it didn't look much like Venice, the real Venice. The houses were contemporary, and the only boats on the water were kayaks and rowboats. Nary a gondola in sight.

They wandered down Ocean Front Walk, the paved path that ran along the sandy beachfront, past the shacks selling t-shirts and knockoff designer sunglasses, the food stalls selling ice cream and fried fish. Street performers, painters, panhandlers. Loud reggae blasted from a speaker somewhere. Plenty of weed, the smell always heavy in the air in the afternoon.

Troy liked the area more than Vish did. She dragged him into dingy, cluttered shops and stood elbow to elbow with tourists while she admired shell necklaces and cheap bangle bracelets. Vish, who had a limited tolerance for shopping, often opted to loiter outside on the pavement while she browsed. He stared at the glistening, muscle-bound specimens working out on the fitness equipment at Muscle Beach and wondered, not for the first time, about Kelsey's claim that Troy usually preferred beefheads.

At one of the shops, Vish bought a necklace for Troy, a blown glass bauble shaped like a tiny bottle. It cost him seven bucks. Troy hugged him and slipped the cheap aluminum chain around her neck, fingering the bottle with as much admiration as if it'd been a diamond pendant.

When they were heading home, when the sun was low and red in the sky above the water, he saw the surfers again, the same pack in Hawaiian shirts and board shorts they'd spotted in Hermosa, loitering around a drinking fountain at the side of the path. Vish paused.

"Maybe we should walk on the sand," he said. He tried to sound nonchalant.

Troy glanced at him, confused, then noticed the surfers. "Why? Because of them?"

"They're the same ones from before, aren't they?"

"Could be. I don't remember what they looked like." Troy looked a little exasperated. "Vish, they're harmless. They're *surfers*. At worst, they'll say something nasty, which… big deal, right?"

She was right, of course. He forced himself to smile at her. "Yeah. Sorry."

They walked past. The surfers didn't say anything this time, but their conversation stopped. Even though their eyes were hidden behind sunglasses, Vish somehow knew, knew they were staring after them. And it frightened him.

CHAPTER TWELVE

COSTUMES WERE REQUIRED for Kelsey's party, even though Halloween was more than two weeks away. Their costumes were not a collaborative effort; Troy took firm control, shooting down all of Vish's suggestions and pushing through her own concept.

"There'll be a red carpet," she said. "And photographers. We can't just half-ass it. This'll be a whole-ass effort or nothing."

Vish would be happier with the "nothing" side of the equation. Troy had procured an elaborate Indian-prince costume for him consisting of a vest and baggy pants in embroidered purple-and-gold satin, a matching turban, and gold sandals. She insisted on painting his eyes, rimming them with her black liquid eyeliner and applying multiple coats of mascara. Vish felt like an ass, and he couldn't help thinking this whole business maybe wasn't a benchmark moment for cultural sensitivity.

Troy looked great, though. She wore some kind of gladiator getup. A sexy gladiator, clad in a gold breastplate and a short gold skirt. Heeled gold sandals that laced up to her knees, a matching sword and shield. The sword was real; Vish had hefted it, and it was heavy and sharp and probably nothing that could be legally carried in public. She wore the glass bottle necklace, as always, even though it looked silly with her costume. Nice to think something he'd given her meant so much to her.

"Where'd you get the outfits?" he asked.

"Called in a few favors with the costume department at the studio," she said. She fussed with a curling iron in his bathroom mirror, turning her blunt bob into a mass of tangled ringlets, which she piled high on her head and secured with a rigid gold headband that resembled a crown. "It's all production wardrobe, from movies or whatever. Aren't they fabulous?"

Troy arranged for a limo to pick them up. Black and sleek and long, it looked out of place waiting at the curb in this neighborhood. Vish had never ridden in one before. It seemed excessive and silly, much like their costumes, but Troy assured him this was a limo-appropriate occasion.

On the way to the Moroccan restaurant where Kelsey's party was taking place, they got tipsy off of the adorable single-serving bottles of champagne stocked in the limo's mini-fridge. That was for the best, because by the time they reached West Hollywood, Vish had managed to overcome his mortification and in fact was feeling pretty warm and good about the whole affair. Champagne was a wondrous elixir.

There was no red carpet, just a line of photographers and a few reporters leading up to the entrance. Vish trailed Troy and remained silent, a dumb smile plastered on his face, as she posed for photos and gave short, funny answers to shouted questions. A bouncer at the door checked their names against a list before gesturing for them to go inside.

Gauzy purple drapes hung from the ceiling and divided the main room of the restaurant into separate areas. Booths of dark wood with carved high backs were partitioned off with embroidered curtains that could be closed for privacy. The tables were tiled with colorful mosaics; hammered bronze lamps mounted to the walls gave off a flickering light.

The room was full of costumed guests. Troy's instincts had been correct; everyone had gone all-out with their attire. As ridiculous as Vish felt, he blended right in.

Just inside the door, Vish stopped in his tracks. There, by the bar. A face he recognized. Dark hair, longish in front, a charcoal suit and white collarless shirt. No tie, no costume unless it was something too subtle for Vish to figure out at a glance. Sparky Mother.

Huh. Well, it made some sense he'd be there. Sparky and Kelsey had clearly known each other at Maryanne's party.

Sparky scanned the crowd, looking bored. His eyes met Vish's, and Vish felt an odd sort of electric charge, but Sparky turned away without changing his expression.

Troy touched his arm. She looked at Sparky. "You know him?" she asked.

"I think so," Vish said. "I don't know if you remember me mentioning him. That's Sparky Mother. He's this manager who offered to look at my writing, but I lost contact with him."

"You should go and talk to him," Troy said.

He was about to mention that it looked like Sparky didn't remember him when they were interrupted by the birthday girl. Kelsey was celebrating her induction into adulthood by dressing as a Disney princess in a gown made from yards and yards of sparkling yellow chiffon bundled up with an enormous poofy satin bow at the back. She threw her arms around Troy and squeezed her tightly. With luck, she wouldn't accidentally impale herself on Troy's sword. "Troy! Vish! I'm so glad you guys could make it! You look fantastic!" She detangled herself from Troy and pulled back so she could better see their costumes. "Oh my gosh! I love Aladdin! You look so awesome!" she said to Vish.

It was easiest just to smile and compliment Kelsey on her own costume, which is what Vish did.

"Have you had anything to eat yet? They're coming around with trays, but the buffet table's over there." Kelsey waved a tiny hand toward the back of the room. "I thought this place would be perfect for my party, looks-wise, but the food here is kind of gross. So I asked the chefs to make all my favorites."

Troy scoped out the contents of a passing tray, which was borne by a white-garbed server. "Which is why we're having sliders at a Moroccan restaurant. Good plan, Kels."

"I can't help it. I like hamburgers, and it's my party." Kelsey giggled. "Help yourselves, guys. I'll be back in a bit." She moved on in a whirl of chiffon to greet some new arrivals.

Vish slid Troy a sidelong glance. "You didn't deliberately dress me as Aladdin, did you?"

"Please. Perish the thought." Troy craned her head around the room. "Is the bar open, or are the paparazzi deterring this place from serving alcohol at a teenager's birthday party?"

"There's a bar. What do you want? More champagne?"

"Whatever you're having. Thanks." Troy kissed him on the nose. "Ridpath's here. I'm going to go say hi while you suss out the drink situation."

Vish squeezed into an empty spot at the bar and waited for the bartender to work his way down to his end. Someone jostled his elbow. He glanced over. Sparky.

Sparky looked straight ahead, forearms resting on the bar, his attention fixed on the wall. When he spoke, it took Vish a minute to realize his words were directed at him.

"I got your message," Sparky said. "Sorry I didn't get back to you. I've been busy." He glanced at Vish once, quickly, then looked forward again. "You look ridiculous, by the way."

Vish was startled into silence for a moment. "It's a costume party, if you've noticed. And I didn't leave you a message," he said at last.

"You called, though."

"I tried. The number you gave me wasn't working."

"It works. It's just… monitored." Sparky's mouth twisted into a quick grimace. "Things are a little dicey right now. Everything okay with you?"

Monitored? That phone call that never quite reached Sparky's office, the whispering void and static on the line…"Yeah. Everything's great."

Sparky threw a quick glance around the room. "Yeah, well, about that," he said. "Things are most definitely not great for you, and that's kind of entirely my fault."

"What?"

"I got you into a lot of trouble. Sorry about that, but if you do whatever I tell you, everything's going to be fine, probably." Sparky looked at him. For the first time, Vish noticed his eyes were a very dark blue, framed by those thick, dark lashes. "She'll kill you if she can."

"What?" Vish said again. "Who?"

Sparky glanced over Vish's shoulder, then grimaced. He shook his head. "I'll be in touch. Take care of yourself, Vish." And with a pat on Vish's arm, Sparky withdrew into the crowd.

Vish jumped at a light hand on his shoulder. Troy. She looked startled by his reaction. "Just checking to see how you're coming on the drinks," she said. She glanced around. "Were you talking to your manager friend?"

Vish almost denied it, though he didn't know why. "Just for a second," he said.

She'll kill you if she can.

"I need to hit the ladies' room," Troy said. "At this rate, you'll probably still be here by the time I'm done."

She melted off into the crowd again. The bartender wasn't anywhere close to his end of the bar, so Vish just snagged two slender flutes of champagne from a tray carried by a passing waiter, then did a quick reconnoiter of the room in search of Sparky. No sign of him.

The explosion shook the restaurant. A low boom, a vibration that rattled the lanterns on the walls, and then smoke poured into the dining area from somewhere in the back, puffy gray clouds that bore an acrid scent.

A moment of stunned silence, and then pandemonium erupted.

Someone slammed into Vish from behind. The champagne glasses went flying out of his hands. Costumed party guests swarmed past him en masse toward the front of the restaurant. He grabbed the bar to brace himself against the flow of bodies. Troy. Troy was in the ladies room, which was at the back of the restaurant, which was where the explosion came from…

Chaos. Screams and shouts. Stampeding guests, their dazzling costumes in disarray, knocked each other over and upended tables and ripped drapes down from the ceiling in their crazed attempts to get outside. Broken glasses and smashed plates of half-eaten food littered the floor.

A hand on his wrist. Vish turned and saw Troy, safe and sound. Her color was high; her eyes glittered with excitement. "There you are. Crap. What happened?" she asked. She looked around.

He pulled her into his arms and clutched her against him. "I don't know. It was an explosion. Were you close to it?" he asked. "I thought you might have been caught in it. I was looking for you."

"I'm fine. I'm okay. I didn't see anything. I was in the ladies' room, and I heard some kind of bang. Maybe something in the kitchen blew up. Gas stove, maybe." She squirmed out of his grip and reached up to straighten his turban. "It smells terrible in here. Let's get away from the smoke or whatever this shit is."

They had to wait for the congestion at the door to clear. Vish, jittery with adrenaline, wanted to push and claw his way out with the other guests, but Troy, ever calm and collected, linked her fingers with his and anchored him to one spot.

They were among the last to evacuate. The night air was crisp and cold. Vish shivered in his vest. Troy, in her skimpy metal breastplate, didn't seem affected by the chill.

Everyone stood on the sidewalk in confused clumps, the pretty costumes sad and incongruous on the city street. A fire truck arrived, followed by an ambulance and two police cars. While the firemen swarmed into the restaurant, a police officer addressed the crowd.

"Folks, we're going to need you to stay here for just a little bit longer while we investigate the situation," he said. He was burly and middle-aged, with a red beard and redder cheeks. "Who here can tell me exactly what happened?"

"There was a bang." That was Kelsey. Her face was pink and puffy, and it was obvious she'd been crying. One of the photographers darted right in front of her and snapped a picture inches from her nose; Kelsey blinked in confusion from the flash, but didn't turn away. "And then there was smoke, and it smelled bad, and everyone started screaming." Her voice broke, and she started crying again. Troy instinctively moved toward her, but two girls in princess costumes flanking Kelsey wrapped their arms around their friend. Kelsey buried her face into their gauzy dresses and sobbed.

"Crappy birthday party, huh?" Troy said under her breath to Vish. "Poor kid."

Vish nodded. He looked around at the other evacuated party guests. No sign of Sparky.

In turn, a calm, polite police officer took down their names and their accounts of the incident. After just under an hour of loitering on the sidewalk in the cold night air, they were given the go-ahead to leave. Good. Vish's sandals were killing him by this point, and he could only imagine what Troy's feet felt like. Troy called their driver to summon their limo, and they slid into the warm, comfortable interior.

As soon as the door was shut behind them, safe in the cream leather cocoon, Vish felt better. "What do you think happened?" he asked.

Troy shrugged. "Some weird accident, I guess," she said. "I'm just glad it wasn't anything serious."

"Are we going to my place?" Vish asked.

"You bet." Troy leaned forward and consulted with the driver through the tiny window. When she sat back, the screen rolled up to give them further privacy.

She grinned. "Ever done it in a limo?"

Before Vish could protest that sex in public places wasn't his kink—in fact, he found the idea off-putting—she was on him, unhooking her sword and letting it fall to the carpeted floor. She settled over his lap and propped her arms against the seat behind him. She unfastened his loose silk trousers and lifted up her short gold skirt. A few adjustments were made, and then she rode him, her cheeks flushing, her curls tumbling out of her upswept hairdo.

Vish slid his arms up around her bare neck. At some point during the evening she must've lost the glass bottle necklace.

After they were done, she collapsed in his arms. They fixed their clothing and cleaned up with a stack of cocktail napkins from the mini-bar. Troy nestled against him, her breastplate gouging into his chest, and kissed his chin.

"Thank you," she said.

Vish smiled. "What for?" he asked. "You did all the hard work."

"For everything," Troy said. "It's been a fun evening."

Considering the excitement at Kelsey's party, "fun" wasn't the right word, but the burst of panic and confusion now seemed trivial compared to the reality of Troy in his arms. Vish snuggled her closer to him, ignoring the pain in his ribs, and closed his eyes.

CHAPTER THIRTEEN

TROY VANISHED THE next morning. Vish woke up alone in his bed, and there was no sign of her. It was still dark in his bedroom. He squinted at the clock. Just after six.

He pulled on his bathrobe and ventured into the living room. Troy kept odd hours, thanks to her television schedule, and it wasn't uncommon for her to rise early and make coffee, then sit by herself on the couch, reading a magazine while patiently waiting for him to wake up.

She wasn't there. Strange that she'd leave without telling him. She hadn't mentioned anything she needed to do this morning—no auditions, no errands, no appointments. Maybe she'd run out to grab breakfast.

No. She'd taken her gladiator costume with her. Presumably she wasn't wearing it right now, which meant she'd changed into the clothes she kept in Vish's room. He checked.

Gone.

Everything of hers was gone, the small armful of sweatshirts and underwear and leggings she'd stashed in one of his dresser drawers.

Huh. That was odd, odd enough to give him an uneasy prickle in his chest. But they'd had a great evening together, all sex and giggles, despite the bizarre events at Kelsey's party, so it wasn't like Troy had left permanently.

He called her. Her phone rang five times, then went to voicemail. He paused, about to leave a message, then hung up instead.

He measured grounds into the coffee pot and tried not to worry.

He didn't hear from Troy all day.

He called her two more times, leaving artfully breezy voicemails. He needed groceries, but he stayed home, struck by a sense of foreboding, some kind of homing instinct that compelled him to stay indoors.

He read online reports about Kelsey's party. The explosion hadn't been important enough to warrant more than a quick mention in the national news, but the gossip sites were all over it. It was a stink bomb, they claimed, a juvenile prank, likely planted by one of Kelsey's former 'tween-star rivals. Speculation as to the perpetrator was rife. No one had been injured, and the general consensus seemed to be that it was all pretty lame. Vish watched some blurry video footage of evacuated party guests standing outside the restaurant; he caught a brief, fuzzy glimpse of Troy standing next to him, and it made him feel melancholy.

Troy finally answered her phone the next morning. Her voice sounded thin and uncertain, and this scared him almost as much as her words.

"I'm sorry I didn't get back to you yesterday," she said. "I just…" She trailed off. Vish heard her inhale on the other end of the line, a million miles away from him, then try again. "I just didn't feel well."

"What's wrong? Are you sick?" he asked. "Troy, is everything okay?"

"Everything's fine. I think I caught a cold or something." She paused, then her words came out in a tumbled rush. "I don't want to see you anymore."

Vish was stunned into silence. "Why?" he finally asked.

"It's just… it's not working out," she said.

"Did I do something?" His voice sounded calm and level, which was odd, because he was screaming inside.

"No. Not really. It's…" She made some kind of noise, an indeterminate sigh. "I don't think I can explain. I just don't want to see you again. Ever."

"Can we meet to talk about this?" he asked. Still calm.

"I don't think so," she said. A long pause, during which Vish felt his heart crumble. "Goodbye." She disconnected the call.

Vish held his phone to his ear with cold fingers and listened to the dial tone. From the start, he'd expected Troy to exit his life as swiftly as she'd entered, but not like this. She would've been kind about it, full of brisk reassurances that it wasn't anything he'd done, that they'd keep in touch, that he'd find someone better for him soon. That was Troy, not that uncertain, inarticulate creature on the phone.

Not really. What had he done? How had he ruined things?

He almost called her again. Some remaining scrap of pride prevented him from hitting the redial button. She wouldn't answer. She'd spent all of yesterday avoiding his calls; she hadn't wanted to talk to him now, though she'd probably figured it'd be better to cut him out of her life now than spend the next several days dodging him.

Later that day, the flu struck, an especially pernicious and incapacitating strain. He spent the evening sitting on the bathroom floor, clutching his stomach, staying within easy barfing distance of the toilet.

He sweated and vomited. He sat in the shower, knees to his chest, and let hot water pound down on him, too shaky to stand up and too exhausted to shave or shampoo his hair. He made endless cups of herbal tea that he never touched, because even a tiny swallow would start him vomiting again. He nibbled on unbuttered toast. He cried a lot, alone in his bed, and felt feeble and ridiculous for it.

He didn't leave his apartment for three days.

On the fourth day, he ran out of tea. He didn't have anything stronger than aspirin on hand, and he needed something that would dull the ache in his bones, would dry up the thick mucous that had staged a hostile takeover of his upper respiratory system, would help him get some badly-needed sleep. He pulled a sweatshirt over the sweatpants he used as pajama bottoms, slid on his sandals, and headed on foot to the grocery store.

It was cold outside. Every time he breathed in, the chill in the air seared his lungs, and he'd explode into a paroxysm of coughing. His throat was nothing but swollen, shredded tissue. His mouth tasted of blood.

He got lost along the way, and he ended up stumbling around the canals, which turned into a maze designed to confound him. The water in the canals had gone green and

120

foamy and stank of rotting fish. Vish gripped the railing of one of the quaint wooden bridges and didn't inhale or look down, because the sight and smell of the water made his stomach clench.

At the grocery store, where he clutched his basket with both hands and tried not to sway on his feet, Vish ran into Mariposa. He was focusing so intently on picking up the handful of items on his shopping list and returning home without incident that he failed to recognize her, until she stood right in front of him and waved with both hands to get his attention.

"Hey, you," she said. She was resplendent in an electric blue parka with a pink fur collar over a denim skirt and flip-flops. "Did you walk here? I could have given you a ride."

"Hi, Mariposa."

She looked into his basket and spotted the orange juice, the cans of soup, the virulent green cold medicine, the extra-large box of tissues. "Oh, you've got that, huh?"

"What?"

She shrugged. "Whatever's going around. Mama's got it, everyone's got it. Some kind of flu or whatever."

"Don't get too close. I don't want to spread it," Vish said.

She rolled her eyes. "I'm immune, seriously. If I don't have it by now, I'm not going to get it, right?" She observed him for a moment, her mouth twisting in concern. Vish hadn't looked in a mirror for a few days. He probably looked like death. "Come on. If you're done here, I can give you a ride home."

He wasn't done, not quite, but he was in no shape to decline the offer. He paid for his groceries, the checkout process seeming ridiculously complicated. Mariposa whisked the bag of purchases out of his arms before he could protest and guided him to her car, which had a crumpled fender and the handle fasted to the passenger door by a gigantic wad of duct tape. She stashed his groceries in her trunk and got in. "Put your seat belt on," she told him. "And don't tell my mother about this. I promised her I wouldn't give any rides to boys, otherwise she'll take the car away."

"I promise."

She drove toward their building. "You still with that girl?" she asked. "The one with the reddish hair?"

"No." Vish almost burst into tears just saying that, his first public acknowledgment that Troy was no longer a part of his life. "She's gone."

"Sorry. I guess. Are you sorry about it?"

"Yes. I am," he said.

"She looked kind of snotty. Was she snotty?"

"No. She was nice." Vish closed his eyes and leaned his head against the door. The glass of the window was cool against his forehead.

Mariposa was quiet for a while. Then: "You know there's something living in that hole?"

His brain wasn't at its best these days. As much as he tried, he couldn't make sense of that. He straightened up and looked at her. "What?"

"The hole in the corner of the building. From the earthquake, remember? There's something in it. I've seen something moving in there, lots of times."

"Probably rats. Or possums," Vish said. "I've seen possums in the neighborhood before."

"Yeah." Mariposa didn't sound convinced. "But the weird thing is, I've shone a flashlight around in there. Like, there's a shadow, and the shadow moves, but there's nothing causing the shadow."

Vish looked at her, confused. "There must be something," he said.

"I know." She frowned. She pulled into her assigned space in front of the gate. "I guess, but it doesn't seem like it."

They walked toward the stairs. Vish looked at the crumbled corner, which was still blocked off with an orange safety cone. Mariposa glanced over at it too. Her brow creased.

"I don't like looking at it. It scares me." She shrugged. "Mama says I'm being stupid."

She probably was being stupid. So was Vish, because he didn't like looking at it either.

"You should stay away from it. Might be dangerous," he said. He tried to make his voice nonchalant. "If there's rats or something, I mean. You could get rabies."

Mariposa gave him a sidelong glance, like she knew he was full of crap. "You too," she said.

It seemed like good advice.

CHAPTER FOURTEEN

AFTER SIX DAYS of misery, Vish felt well enough to visit Troy. He tried calling first and she didn't pick up, so he decided to take a chance and stop by unannounced. She might not even be home, but Troy's Saturdays were generally leisurely, especially now that she wasn't working. If he could just see her...

He took a bus down the coast to Hermosa. Inside a paper bag in his lap rested the excuse for his visit, a pair of cobalt ballet flats she'd left at his apartment. He felt awful—still weak, still sore, still headachey—but he hadn't vomited in over a day, and thus he must be on the mend.

He made his way down to the beach and wandered along the Strand until he found the right house. There was no doorbell, so he rapped on the sliding door.

A figure approached from inside. Vish's heart beat faster, until he realized it was Lola. She stared at him through the glass, then slid the door open a few inches.

"Hey," she said. "She's not here. She's at an audition."

"She left these at my place," he said. He held up the flats.

Lola stared at them. Vish expected her to take them and close the door, but instead she opened it a bit wider and craned her head outside. She looked around in both directions, then ducked back and slid the door fully open. "Go ahead and come in," she said.

Vish stepped inside. Lola closed the door behind him and pulled the drapes across it, blocking the view of the beach.

"She'll be gone all morning, probably, but I don't need the neighbors telling her you stopped by." She nodded at the shoes in his hand. "Keep them or throw them. I'm not taking them, because she'll know you were here, and that's a conversation I don't want to have."

"I don't understand," Vish said. "Do you know why she broke up with me?"

Lola stared at him. She looked like she had just woken up, all tangled hair and puffy eyes. "You're not going to cry, are you? I can't deal with a crying man today."

She padded barefoot over to the kitchen. She wore only a threadbare black sweater, barely long enough to function as a dress, her legs pale beneath it. Cobwebs of purple veins covered her skinny white thighs. She yanked open the refrigerator and stared inside. "You want water or something?"

"No. Thank you," Vish said. "Can you tell me why Troy left me?"

She straightened up, a water bottle clutched in her hand. She looked exasperated. "Because Troy is a goddamned flake," she said.

She slammed the fridge shut and walked over to the couch. "Sit," she said.

Vish perched on the edge of a cushion, the unwanted shoes balanced on his knees. Lola plopped down beside him. She rolled her eyes. "I mean, she's a friend and I love her, but she's always been a flake. And it's cool for the most part, but I think you got screwed in the process."

"What do you mean?" Vish asked.

She exhaled. "Here's the situation. Appreciate this, because Troy would be pissed at me if she knew I was even talking to you. And if it ever comes out you treated her wrong or were a jerk to her in any way, you know I'll have your balls, right?" She shrugged. "But you seem like a nice guy. Not Troy's normal thing at all, but I have to say, she was better with you. Nicer to people, less swept up in her own personal drama. Less of a bitch, I guess is what I'm saying."

She settled back on the couch and took a swig of water. "So a week ago, she comes home in the morning, and it's the same goddamned Troy back. She's in tears. I thought you might have done something shitty to her, but she told me you hadn't. But…" She stopped.

"But what?" Vish asked. "Why did she leave me?"

"She said you must have somehow tricked her into dating you," Lola said. "She thought you might be evil. That's a quote, by the way."

Whatever Vish was expecting, that wasn't it. "What?"

"I don't know, so don't go asking me to explain it. That's pretty much all she said, and when I pressed her, she didn't give specifics. Just cried a lot." Lola shook her head. "And *that*, my love, is a whole lot like the Troy I know."

Vish stared at her. "Funny," he said. "Because that's nothing like the Troy I know."

Lola shrugged. "I don't know what to tell you. Either you brought out something different in her, or she was putting on an act to impress you. Or maybe you just saw whatever you wanted to see in her."

"So what do I do now?"

"I don't really care, as long as it doesn't involve Troy." At his expression, something in Lola's face softened. "Look, she doesn't want to see you. She's not going to meet with you or take your calls. Move on. Whatever you thought about her, you have to accept that it's over, because there's nothing you can do about it."

There was nowhere to go from there. He could argue that no, he knew the real Troy, and Troy loved him, or was fond enough of him that she'd never claim he was evil, for crying out loud, but there was nothing to be gained by it. In the end, he just left.

He couldn't face the bus, so he walked north along the shore, sticking close to the water's edge through the vast industrial void of El Segundo. He trudged along the grassy stretch of Dockweiler Beach while low jets roared overhead from neighboring LAX, then detoured too far off his course through the maze of docks in Marina Del Rey. He considered stuffing Troy's shoes in a trash can, but they were in good shape and were probably expensive, so he left them on a bench. Maybe someone could use them.

He kept walking. Found his way back to the shoreline. Didn't run into many people. It was a weekend, but it was a foggy fall day, and nobody wanted to spend it at the beach.

This might be a bad idea, walking around. He felt weak and dizzy. He inhaled too much of the chilly ocean air and erupted into a coughing fit, and his nose turned into a spigot of mucous. Great. His chest had been tight ever since he'd talked to Lola. Maybe it was from his illness, or maybe he just needed to have another good cry, because now he knew he'd lost Troy for good.

The attack came right when he'd reached the south end of Venice, just beyond the fishing pier. Someone slammed into his back with enough force to knock the breath out of him and tackled him to the ground. He choked and coughed, his tortured lungs unable to get enough oxygen. His assailant pressed against the back of the head and forced his face into the sand.

He twisted and bucked and tried to push himself up off the ground. He turned his head to look at his attacker, and an elbow slammed into his temple. Before his vision exploded into white light, he caught a blurred glimpse of tanned arms and a brightly-patterned shirt.

Someone kicked him in the side. Pain burst throughout his ribs. He rolled onto his hip and tried to scramble away, but another kick caught him between his shoulder blades, then another to the back of his head.

Multiple attackers. The band of surfers. They were on him, four of them, snarling and spitting, feral in their aggression. They hit him and kicked him, no sense to any of it. Vish tried to raise his hands to defend himself, tried to curl into a protective ball, but the blows came too fast from too many directions.

One of them said something, but he couldn't catch more than a general sense of the words: "He can't reach you here." Something like that.

"This is too public." That was the one he guessed was the leader, the dark-haired one with the handsome features. "Get him out of here."

One of the surfers grabbed both his wrists and yanked on his arms. Another went for his ankles, but Vish kicked for all he was worth, lashing out at bare legs and kneecaps. He tried to shout for help and erupted into another coughing fit.

"Hey! Hey!" A male voice, loud and angry. The surfers paused their attack and looked up. Vish broke the slackened grip of the one holding his wrists.

"Get away from him! What are you doing?" Vish looked up. A guardian angel in a white t-shirt and red shorts sprinted across the sand toward him.

The surfers scattered in all directions. Vish saw the dark-haired one running across the sand toward Ocean Front Walk. The kid in the red shorts took a couple of tentative steps after him, then stopped. He sank to his knees in the sand next to Vish. A tanned face, young and clean-cut and earnest with concern and outrage, stared down at Vish.

"Are you okay?" the kid asked. His hair, which was probably naturally brown, was bleached to a pale beige by the sun; dark freckles stood out across his nose and forehead. "Are you hurt? Don't move if you're hurt."

"I think I'm okay." Vish started to sit up. The kid looked like he was going to tell him to keep still, then slipped his arm around Vish's back and helped him. His white t-shirt had a red cross on it. Ah. The kid was a lifeguard.

"Who were those guys? Why were they beating you?" the kid asked. He was maybe nineteen or twenty, California-handsome and adorably earnest. "Did you break anything? Do you need an ambulance?"

His chest hurt, but that was as much from the week of nonstop coughing as the kicks he'd received. The surfers had worn sandals, which hadn't inflicted all that much damage. He'd be bruised all over, but everything considered, he'd gotten off lightly. "I'm fine," he said.

He tried to stand. His arm still around Vish, the kid helped him to his feet. "Did they mug you?"

Vish touched his back pocket. His wallet was still there. "No. Maybe they didn't get around to it." He looked at the kid. "Thank you for saving me."

The kid grinned. "My job," he said. He pointed a short distance ahead to a squat beige structure on the sand. It was topped by a short tower with a glass-walled observation deck that ran along all sides. "That's the lifeguard HQ. Can you make it there? There's a medic on duty, and I want him to look at you."

"That's not necessary," Vish said. "Thank you, but I'd rather just go home."

"I have to file a report." The kid looked abashed. "It's part of my job. And you should have someone check you out. I'm not kidding. You had four dudes whaling on you."

Vish hesitated, then nodded. "Okay. Sure." One of these days he was going to learn how to put his foot down and take a stand against all these kind, considerate people who kept wanting to send him to doctors.

The kid took his arm and led him up the beach, like a good-natured grandson taking his doddering grandfather for a stroll. "Do you know why they jumped you? Did they say anything?"

Vish shook his head. "I think I've seen them before, though. Once around here, by the shops, and once down in Hermosa."

"I've never seen them on this beach. They're not regulars, at least."

They made it to the building. Inside, it was roomy and clean. The kid guided him to a small white examination room and gestured toward a padded cot. "Have a seat, okay? I'm going to see who's around."

Vish stared at the laminated CPR posters taped to the walls until the kid returned a couple minutes later. He was accompanied by an LAPD officer. She looked young and grimly competent, with her dark hair pulled into a smooth bun. In spite of the chill in the air, she wore a short-sleeved uniform shirt paired with shorts. Her utility belt sagged under the weight of its load: holstered gun, walkie-talkie, handcuffs, mace.

"We radioed for the nurse. He's treating someone at the north end of the beach right now, but he'll be here soon as he's done," she said to Vish. "I'm Officer Guerrero. Kip said he saw you get attacked?"

Kip. Vish almost smiled. The lifeguard looked like a Kip. "Yes. I was out walking, and four guys ambushed me from behind."

Officer Guerrero took a small notebook and a ballpoint pen out of her back pocket. She leaned against the wall. "So you don't have any idea why they attacked you?" she asked.

She sounded completely neutral, like she neither believed nor disbelieved him, and yet Vish felt himself striving to sound more convincing.

"No, ma'am," he said. He thought she winced at the "ma'am." "Like I told Kip earlier, I think I've seen them around before, but I don't know why they'd beat me up."

"Where was this?"

"Once in the South Bay, once around here. I was just out walking with my girlfriend both times. The first time, they said something to me, but we pretty much just ignored them."

"Yeah? What'd they say?"

"I don't remember exactly. One of them said something about how I was a dead man. 'Dead man walking.' Something like that."

Her brows raised. "Well, that seems significant."

"Yeah, but it didn't sound like he was threatening to kill me. It wasn't like he was angry at me or anything. He and his friends were just hanging out, and I think he wanted to get under my skin a little."

"Yeah, well, mission accomplished." Officer Guerrero scrawled in her notepad. "Your girlfriend know them? Maybe had some kind of problem with them that you don't know about?"

"She said she didn't know them," Vish said.

Guerrero looked at him and her expression sharpened. She'd zeroed in on his words, pinpointed his uncertainty. "That might've been what she said, but did she?"

Vish shook his head. "I don't think so. They weren't the type of people she'd know."

She stared at him, unblinking, for far too long. Vish fought an urge to fill the silence with nervous chatter. Finally, she flipped to a blank sheet and passed her notebook and pen to him. "Give me her name and info," she said. "We can check with her."

Vish hesitated. "Do you have to?" he asked. "We broke up recently."

This earned him another unblinking stare, this once laced with a blast of ice. "Her name and number, please."

With a sinking feeling, Vish scribbled down Troy's name and her cell number. Maybe Troy would repeat what she'd told Lola about thinking Vish was evil. That'd go over well with grim Officer Guerrero.

He handed the notebook back. She jotted down his vague, jumbled physical description of the surfers, copied his personal information from his drivers license, asked a few general questions about the incident.

"Sorry you had that experience," she said. "Haven't heard of any similar problems lately, but we'll be on the lookout."

"Thank you."

She hesitated. "Your girlfriend… Any chance she could be behind the attack? Maybe carrying a grudge about something?"

"No," Vish said. "It's not in her nature. She wouldn't do anything like that." Guerrero nodded thoughtfully.

The nurse arrived as they were wrapping up. He was a burly man with massive forearms bulging out from a tight white polo shirt. He gave Vish a once-over, shone a bright light in his eyes, made him flex his arms and wrists and legs, and gave him the all-clear. "You're good," he said. "You got anyone to drive you home?"

Vish shook his head. "I'm just a few blocks from here," he said, or tried to say. He erupted into a coughing fit mid-sentence. The nurse gave him a whack on the back with a beefy hand.

"Sounds like you got what everyone's got. Bad strain of flu going around," he said.

"Getting over it," Vish said.

"Lucky you. Most people are just catching it now," the nurse said. "If it keeps spreading like this, it'll knock out the whole city."

Vish walked home. He felt newly exposed after the attack, frightened by the wide expanses of sand and water around him. He felt better once he was on the street, sheltered by the upscale, sprawling apartment complexes and oceanfront hotels that dotted the area. What had they said? *He can't reach you here.*

He shouldn't expect that to make any sense. He was a random victim, or mostly random, someone they'd slotted into some sort of paranoid fantasy that drove them to attack him.

Maybe they hadn't said "he". He'd been with Troy both times when he'd seen them before. "She can't protect you"— now that Troy wasn't around, maybe he was fair game? Was that a completely bizarre thing to think, that somehow Troy was involved in this?

Sparky Mother had warned him about Troy, or about someone at least, and then there'd been that explosion, and then immediately after that Troy had vanished from his life.

And now he'd been attacked. Random events, or was there some connection he was missing?

Troy was a dead end. He could try ambushing her at her duplex again, but she'd just refuse to see him. Sparky, though... maybe he could find Sparky again, and maybe Sparky held some of the answers in this.

It was a relief to get home, to pull the blinds shut, to flip the double bolt and put the chain lock on the door. He pulled Sparky's business card out of the junk drawer in his kitchen where he'd stashed it a couple weeks ago. That logo, the stupid cartoon tiger with the firecracker.

He dialed the number again.

Again, no connection. No ringing, no dial tone, just an electronic void. A rising and falling pulse, a series of far-away clicks, like an electronic echo. But Sparky had known he'd called before...

"It's Vish," he said into the dead line. He felt like an idiot. "I'd like to speak to you."

The void didn't respond. He listened to the echo for a few seconds longer, then hung up, feeling foolish and oddly scared.

CHAPTER FIFTEEN

IT WAS TRICKY getting to Ridpath's house in Tarzana on the bus; anything in the Valley was sort of a no-man's-land for people without cars. Vish had pored over the map of the public transit system online before settling on a route he thought would work, and even then he wandered through residential neighborhoods for a couple of miles, consulting the little map he'd printed from the MTA's website and trying to find something that looked familiar from the time he and Troy had gone to Ridpath's barbecue. He didn't have a phone number, or even his full address. He remembered the nearest major intersection, he thought, and he hoped he could navigate his way to the right house from there.

After a few wrong turns, he found the place, a cute two-story cottage in dusty blue with cream trim. There was a lemon tree in the front lawn, graceful and fragrant. He rang the doorbell and heard answering barks. Ridpath had pugs, two of them.

A man's voice spoke something unintelligible. The barking ceased. The door flew open. Ridpath, shirtless and glistening, grinned at him. "Vish!"

"Hi, Ridpath. I'm sorry to just drop by like this. I didn't have any other way to contact you."

"No, it's no problem. I was just doing some free weights. Come on in. Something to drink?"

Vish squeezed in past the dogs, who milled about and sniffed his shins. Ridpath led the way into the kitchen. He glanced back over his shoulder. "Everything okay?"

"Yes. Fine."

"You got a little banged up," Ridpath said.

Vish touched the purple welt on his forehead. His ribs had some yellowing bruises on them, and he felt stiff, but that was the extent of the damage. "I got mugged," he said. He tried to make it sound light.

Ridpath stopped. "No kidding. Really? When did this happen?"

"Day before yesterday. I was walking on the beach in Venice. It's fine. I wasn't badly hurt."

"Was Troy with you?" Ridpath opened the fridge and started rooting around. "Beer, bottled water?"

"Nothing for me. Thank you." Vish watched as Ridpath twisted the cap off a bottle of water and took a long pull from it. "No. Troy and I… we broke up."

Ridpath set the bottle down on the counter and stared at him. "Sorry to hear that," he said at last. "What happened?"

"I don't know, other than it was her idea. She's… not really speaking to me anymore."

"You want to sit down?" Ridpath asked. He gestured for Vish to follow him into the living room. "Well, that's too bad. I thought you two were good together."

"So did I," Vish said. He sank down into an armchair, which absorbed him into its cushiony chenille depths.

Ridpath settled on the couch. His upper body was a triumph of fitness, crisply defined ridges and taut skin, not a visible trace of unwanted flesh anywhere. "Is that what you wanted to talk to me about?"

"No," Vish said. "You're Troy's friend. You know her better than you know me. I don't think it would be appropriate for me to discuss her with you."

Ridpath nodded. "Good call," he said. "So…"

Vish thought this through in advance, rehearsed it in his head during the long bus trip here, made sure it sounded plausible. "I talked to one of the guests at Kelsey's party, this manager, I think he's a friend of hers. He asked me to send him some of my writing, but I lost his phone number."

"And you want me to see if Kelsey has it?"

"If you don't mind, yeah. I hate to ask, but since Troy's not talking to me, I don't know any other way to contact her."

"Sure, no problem. I can do that." He thought for a moment. "This guy doesn't have anything to do with Troy, does he? He's not why she left you?"

"No. Not at all. Nothing like that."

"Good. I like you just fine, but I'm not putting myself in the middle of some messy breakup drama." He smiled. "What's the guy's name?"

"Sparky Mother."

Ridpath snorted. "Easy to remember, I guess. Sparky a nickname?"

"Probably, but as far as I know, everyone calls him Sparky."

Ridpath picked his phone up off of the coffee table and handed it to Vish. "Okay. Give me your phone number, and I'll give you a call when I talk to her."

"Thanks a lot. I appreciate it." Vish entered his information into Ridpath's phone. "Hey, do you think the show's ever coming back?"

"Nope. I think the network's looking for an excuse to let it fade away. This season's been a big embarrassment for them."

Vish nodded. "Are you all right with that?"

"I think so." Ridpath considered. "Steady paycheck, that's awfully nice, but it'll be a relief to be done with it, honestly. I suppose there's a chance the writers will get their act together during this hiatus." He raised his eyebrows at Vish. "Though I'd guess you'd have a better idea about that?"

Vish shook his head. "They won't," he said.

"No surprise there." Ridpath shrugged. "Maybe we'll work together again on something better."

Nice thought, but Vish couldn't see it happening. His job had been an out-of-the-blue fluke, a gift from the skies that had come along with Troy. It seemed very unlikely another such gift would ever come to him again.

Ridpath called the next day. "Sorry for the delay," he said. "Kelsey had to check with her party planner. Anyway, yeah, she knew who you were talking about, this Sparky Mother dude, though she's really just met him at other parties and stuff. She wasn't even sure what he does, other than he's in the industry."

"Did she know how to contact him?"

"Not exactly. Here's the thing: She didn't invite him, or her party planner didn't invite him, or however that works. The invitation went to some big-league agent who couldn't make it, so he passed the invitation along to Sparky. This agent called Kelsey's planner ahead of time and got Sparky on the guest list."

"Who was the agent?" Vish asked.

"His name's Lon Hartford. He used to have his own agency, but he's retired. He represented Kelsey when she was a kid. Or more of a kid, anyway." Ridpath snorted. "He still shows up at events, but he's no longer active in the industry. Maybe your friend Sparky used to work with him or something? Anyway, he'd know how to get in touch with him." Ridpath read off a phone number; Vish jotted it down on the back of a magazine.

"Thanks, Ridpath. I owe you."

"Hell, that wasn't anything. Take care of yourself, Vish."

Ridpath hung up. Vish sat on his couch and stared at the wall, stumped. What was his next move? Was this crazy, chasing down Sparky this way?

He dialed the number. A bright female voice answered, perky yet professional. After Vish fumbled his way through an explanation, she put him on hold for a very long time.

"Mr. Hartford doesn't give out that kind of information out over the phone," she said when she returned.

"Ah." Well, that made sense, didn't it? Lon Hartford didn't know Vish; he had no incentive to give him information about one of his friends, or employees, or whatever Sparky was to him. "I see. Well, thank you."

"But if you were to drop by his home tomorrow after two, he'll be available," the bright voice continued seamlessly.

She rattled off an address. Vish fumbled to grab a pen and write it down. Beachwood Canyon, high in the Hollywood Hills. Tough to reach by bus. "I'll be there. Thank you very much—"

He was talking to a dead line. The efficient woman had already disconnected the call.

Vish searched online for Lon Hartford. What with the nebulous cloud surrounding Sparky Mother, it was comforting to see hundreds of results come back for Hartford, who seemed to be wholly legit. Vish found articles in the trades mentioning his past deals, photos of him at parties, quotes from him in the *Los Angeles Times* speculating on next year's Oscar nominations.

Once again, he Googled Sparky.

One result.

Weird.

CHAPTER SIXTEEN

BY THE TIME he reached Hartford's place, it was almost three. Vish, who was compulsively early by nature, was furious with himself for underestimating how long it would take to get there. He'd given himself an ample cushion of time, he thought, but the journey had sucked up his afternoon. A bus to downtown, a subway to Hollywood, and then on foot into the hills, hiking up twisting roads that snaked in all directions and ended without warning. His map led him astray. He was parched and sweaty by the time he reached the mansion.

He rang a buzzer beside the front gate, which swung open and allowed him access. He walked up a cobblestone circular driveway to a pair of enormous doors flanked by white concrete pillars. Only a single story tall, the mansion sprawled over enough space for four or five more modestly-sized houses. The exterior was painted flat yellow, the color of buttercups, and had a low white concrete porch. The huge windows on either side of the door had no curtains; Vish could see straight through the house, all the way through the sliding doors against the back wall to the swimming pool in the backyard.

Lon Hartford answered the door. He might've been in his seventies, maybe even older, but his deeply-tanned skin was tight and smooth, and his swept-back hair was dark and glistening. In one hand he held a tall glass filled with mint leaves and what could be tea or bourbon. "You must be Vish. Come in, come in. Call me Lon."

Lon ushered him into the house. He clapped Vish on the shoulder, like they'd known each other for years. "I'm sitting out by the pool. Join me for a drink." He wore a pale yellow golf shirt and white linen pants. He was barefoot, and it looked like he'd had a recent pedicure.

Just beyond the front entrance was a dining area. Bare walls and pale wood floors, an enormous white marble dining table surrounded by eight high-backed white leather chairs arranged at evenly-spaced intervals. The dining area connected to the living room with little indication to show where one started and one ended, all part of the same open space.

The living room featured a sofa and two vast armchairs upholstered in a sickly yellow suede, like gigantic pats of warm margarine. A shaggy white rug enveloped the floor. He should've taken his shoes off by the door, followed Lon's lead and gone barefoot, because there was no way he'd be able to walk across that rug without tracking dust from the canyon roads.

Unlike the dining area, the walls in the living room weren't bare. Vish wished they were. Eight oil paintings in total, huge unframed canvases hanging high on the walls, done in vivid pinks and roses and beiges and browns. Headless naked women were featured in all of them, bulging breasts and tiny waists and long, long legs, entwined in erotic positions with each other. The heads looked like they'd been severed just under the chin, a glimpse of cut bone and sawed flesh at the top of the neck stumps.

It was seriously creepy.

Lon glanced at him sideways as they passed, gauging his reaction. Vish kept his face neutral. "Amazing work, isn't it?" Lon said. He raised his glass and saluted the paintings. "Local artist. Talented fellow, divinely gifted. He *worships* the female form."

Though not the female face. Vish made some noise of polite acknowledgement.

They moved on through the sliding doors to the back-yard. The pool glittered in the sunlight, blue and clear. It'd been overcast by the beach; here in the hills, it was sunny and stark, the low sun and cloudless sky conspiring to make Vish feel exposed.

A teenaged girl in a gold-and-green bikini sprawled on her stomach in a lounge chair, eyes closed, the fingertips of one hand stroking the pavement. She glanced up and saw Lon and Vish, then stood and, without a word, moved to a small mobile wet bar set up in the shade by the house. She picked up a set of tongs and flicked ice cubes from a teak bucket into a tall glass. She splashed something from a pitcher over the ice, then padded over and thrust the glass at Vish.

"Ah… thank you," Vish said, but she padded off without acknowledging him. She slipped inside the sliding door and yanked it shut behind her, leaving Vish alone with Lon.

"Sit. Please." Lon gestured toward one of the teak reclin-ers surrounding the pool. He smiled, his teeth flashing white against his tan.

Vish sat on the edge of the recliner. He took a tentative sip of his drink. Iced tea, strong and sticky-sweet, a chemical blast of peach flavoring. Lon pulled around a chair to face him, then sat and beamed at him. "So I hear you're looking for Sparky."

"Yes, sir," Vish said. "I met him at a party a while ago, and he offered to read a book I've written, but I don't have any way to contact him."

Lon nodded. "So you're a writer. Good, good. Work on anything I've heard of?"

"I'm currently writing for *Interstellar Boys*," Vish said. Sort of the truth, more of a lie.

Lon kept nodding. "Good show. Good stuff." Another smile. The skin around his mouth pulled tightly over his chin and cheeks, lending his face a skeletal appearance. He sat back in his chair. "I've known Sparky for an awfully long time. He's got a good eye for talent. If he's interested in you, it probably means you know your craft."

"I don't know that much about him," Vish said. "But he seemed like a pretty cool guy."

The smile twisted a bit. Almost a grimace, and then it relaxed. "He's quite a fellow."

"Did he work with you?" Vish asked.

"He took over from me." Another tight smile. "Took my clients. What the hell. It was time I retire anyway, huh?"

"What does he do, exactly?" Vish asked. "Is he an agent, or a manager, or...?"

"He runs things." Lon looked out over the pool and shook his head. "Runs pretty much everything in this industry, really. If there ever was a man behind the curtain, that's Sparky. He does a hell of a job of it, too. Better than I could, then or now."

"There's so little information about him out there," Vish said.

Lon nodded. "He likes it that way. He controls the flow. It adds to his legend, I suppose."

He was still staring at the pool, his expression distant. Just as Vish wondered if he should say something to fill the void, Lon returned to the present and faced him again.

"Kelsey Kirkpatrick's party. Was he there to see you?"

It took Vish a moment to follow him. "Ah… No. I saw him at the party, but I barely got a chance to talk to him. I first met him about a month before that."

He wasn't sure Lon was even listening to him. "He wanted to go to that party. He asked for my invitation. I wondered why, but it's not the sort of thing I could ask him."

"Why not?" Vish asked. "Wouldn't he have told you?"

"He probably would have. And that's the problem. The more Sparky tells you about his life, the worse off you are." He gestured at Vish with his drink. "Which is why I'm not asking for your story, son. You've got your reasons for finding him, and if he wants to see you, he'll see you, but I don't need to know about it."

Lon took a long drink of his tea, then appeared to reach some conclusion. He nodded to himself.

"He moves his offices a lot. I don't know his current number, if he even has a phone right now, but he's set himself up in the Beverly Center these days. You want to see him, try there."

"The Beverly Center?" Vish frowned. "Are there offices there?"

"That's irrelevant to Sparky. He wants to set up in a place, he'll do it, and the place will adapt to his needs." Lon set his empty glass on the cement beside his chair. "Ask around. Someone should be able to point you in the right direction."

Vish nodded. "Okay. Thank you," he said. He rose.

Lon got to his feet as well. He extended a hand; Vish shook it. Lon's hand was dry and withered, as light as a pile of twigs, and his grip had no power behind it.

"Tell him I helped you," Lon said. His tone was light, but Vish thought he detected something sneaking out behind the words, something tense and almost frantic. "Mention my name, will you? Let him know it was me."

"Of course."

Lon smiled and patted him on the shoulder. He walked with him back into the house, through the living room with the creepy paintings, and out the front door. The gate stood wide open, and just the sight of the road beyond it made Vish feel relieved. This was the kind of place where someone could disappear forever.

When he was safely on the road, ready to retrace his meandering journey back home, he glanced back at the house. Lon was still standing barefoot on the concrete porch and staring after him. Lon waved his glass at him in farewell. Vish returned the wave. His hand trembled.

CHAPTER SEVENTEEN

THE BEVERLY CENTER was a mall, not an office building, and it seemed highly unlikely he'd find Sparky here. Nine stories of poured concrete slathered in dark gray paint, monstrous and looming, taking up an enormous chunk of prime real estate on the easternmost edge of Beverly Hills. A smattering of restaurants on the ground floor, then six levels of parking crowned by three floors of upscale retail establishments. Vish took the escalators to the seventh floor, then stood and stared at the shop displays of luxury goods, uncertain.

Did Lon know what he was talking about? Vish hadn't been here in months, but it looked much the same as his last visit. Shops. No offices.

At the customer service desk, a woman was deep in conversation with the uniformed young man behind the counter. She wore a black suit with an impeccably tailored jacket and high black boots with narrow spike heels. She was tall and Asian, with bobbed hair that gleamed copper in the light, and she looked very familiar.

Of course. Sparky's glamorous friend Poppy, who'd picked him up after the party in the hills, who'd signaled to Vish not to accept Sparky's offer of a ride. The young clerk slid a plastic mail bin overflowing with large padded envelopes across the counter to her. Screenplays, maybe, or manuscripts.

Poppy hoisted the bin. She balanced it on one hip, then headed toward the escalators leading up to the highest levels. A small avalanche of padded envelopes shifted and spilled to the marble floor. She paused, teetering in her boots. Her mouth twitched in irritation.

Vish hurried forward and gathered up the fallen envelopes. The addressee was Poppy Kang, not Sparky, but he was in the right place. He gestured toward the bin. "Do you want me to carry that?" he asked.

She looked at him and smiled. No trace of recognition on her lovely face, not that she'd remember their one fleeting prior encounter. "Thanks. That's very cool of you," she said. She passed the overflowing bin to him. "I'm on the top floor."

He followed her up two flights of escalators. The interior of the Beverly Center was nicer than the exterior, all glass walls and glossy marble floors, open space and skylights. Poppy strode ahead of him, her boots clicking smartly.

Top level. Mostly just the food court, plus a few orphaned shops. There'd once been a movie theater here, Vish had heard, a multiplex, but it'd gone out of business years ago. The entrance had been plastered over to match the seamless white wall on either side, and now there was no sign the theater had ever existed.

Poppy headed toward that white wall. Vish trailed her as she walked straight up to a door he could hardly see, just an outline against all the white. No doorknob. She inserted a key into a white-painted lock and pushed it open.

"This is me," she said. She held the door and gestured for him to enter. "Care to come in, Vish?"

Vish's mouth didn't drop open, but it was close.

"You recognized me," he said at last.

"Sure." Poppy had dimples, like Troy. She groped around the wall just inside the door and flicked on the overhead lights. "I was expecting you. If not today, then sometime soon."

Vish found himself in an unfinished space. No dividing walls, a ceiling lined with exposed pipes and dangling electrical wires, bare floorboards. A desk sat near the door, covered with stacks of screenplays and messy piles of paperwork. Poppy nodded toward the desk. "Just put the mail down there."

Vish shifted aside a tower of scripts to make room for the bin. "Lon Hartford said I might be able to find Sparky here."

"That was optimistic of Lon." Poppy grinned. "Sparky almost never comes to the office these days. You'll have to make do with me. Grab a chair from over there and have a seat." She sat down behind her desk.

Vish saw a stack of collapsed folding chairs resting against the wall. He arranged one in front of the desk and sat.

"I'd offer you something to drink, but the amenities are limited," Poppy said. "There's a Starbucks in the food court if you need anything."

Vish glanced at the bare walls, the lack of furnishings. "Did you just move in?" he asked.

"We've been here three months. This is as settled as we're going to get. Sparky likes to switch offices a lot, so it's never worthwhile to invest too much effort in appearances, especially since he's barely ever here."

She pawed through the stacks of papers on her desk. "You're here somewhere. I was just looking at it last week. Give me a second." She picked something up. "Aha."

She held up an unbound sheaf. It looked about manuscript-length. Vish glanced at the title page.

"That's my book," he said. His voice sounded muffled and strange in the cavernous room, or maybe something had gone wrong with his hearing. The blood rushed in his ears, and he felt kind of dizzy, because Poppy had his book, which he'd never sent to Sparky.

"Sure. You wanted Sparky to read it, right?"

"Yes, I did. But… I didn't send it to him," he said.

Poppy shrugged. "You sent it to someone. Sparky asked me to track it down, I sent out feelers, and some agent or publisher or whoever passed it along to me. No real mystery to it."

"Why didn't you ask me for a copy?" Vish asked.

"Same result either way. My method worked, and I didn't have to bother you. From what I hear, you've been tied up lately with other matters." She placed the manuscript on her desk and flipped through the first few pages. "Sparky hasn't read it yet. He's been meaning to, he keeps saying, but between you and me, he probably never will."

"He didn't sound terribly enthusiastic when I described it to him."

Poppy rolled her eyes skyward. "That's Sparky. If you'd managed to work in a cyborg ninja or a nitrogen tank explosion or something, he would've perked right up. I read it, though," she said. She tapped a finger on the title page. Her nails were long and covered with glossy beige polish. "I liked it. It reads very well. Maybe a little soft for the current market, but there's probably a place for it."

"Thank you," Vish said.

"I've suggested some changes throughout. You want to make them, we'll see if we can get this sucker in the hands of the right publisher."

She passed him the manuscript. Vish flipped through it. It was a mess of red pen marks, no page left untouched. Jotted notes in the margins, crossed-out lines, entire paragraphs covered in scribbles.

Vish picked a page at random and reviewed her changes. She knew what she was doing. His sentences were tightened, his prose was punched up, until it read in a swifter, cleaner, easier rhythm. Just at a glance, it was clear she'd made it better.

Some of her changes, though… Vish looked up at her. "You changed character names?"

"Not all of them."

"Katherine to Kathleen? What difference could that make?"

"On the surface? Not a thing. But on the level I'm working at, it could mean the difference between being published and not being published."

Vish stared, not sure how to express his thoughts without giving offense. She smiled at him.

"If it helps, think of your manuscript as a blueprint, the foundation for something that has yet to be built. What I've done is take the next step toward building it."

"But... it's so arbitrary," Vish said. "Changing one name to another... you can't possibly know this will help my book get published."

"Nothing's certain, of course. Do I know what will increase the chances of selling it, though? Absolutely." She shrugged. "If you work with me and Sparky, we can get you published and make you very, very happy. That's a promise. But I understand you might be reluctant to believe I know what I'm talking about. It's a leap of faith."

"I'm sure you're very good at this, but I don't even know who you are," Vish said. "I don't even know who Sparky is."

Poppy examined him. Her expression seemed fond yet remote, like he was someone's kid brother she'd been tasked with entertaining. "Want to grab a drink with me?"

"I... suppose," Vish said.

"Excellent." Poppy flashed her dimples again. She stood and led the way out of the theater, locking the door behind them.

They took the elevator to the first floor, which put them right in the middle of the parking structure. Vish expected Poppy to head for the sidewalk, maybe to one the restaurants lining La Cienega, but instead she strode toward the back of the parking structure, in the opposite direction of the exit.

She pushed open an unmarked door and led Vish to an enclosed outside courtyard. Gravel covered the ground. A black acrylic bar ran the length of an ugly concrete wall, with a smattering of iron bistro tables shaded with patio umbrellas arranged in front of it.

Two exquisite young men with dark suits and expensive haircuts sat on tall stools at the bar, sipping Scotch and conversing. They glanced back at Poppy and Vish and fell silent for a moment, then resumed their dialogue in hushed tones, their heads close together.

The patio tables were all unoccupied. Poppy sat down at one and gestured for Vish to take the seat across from her. "This okay?" she asked.

"Sure." Vish sat and looked around. "I had no idea this place was here."

"Most people don't," she said. "Nobody goes here who doesn't belong."

"What's that noise?" he asked. It was an electronic hum, omnipresent, not loud but impossible to ignore.

"It's the oil well," Poppy said. At Vish's confused expression, she explained. "The mall is built around an oil well. They put up a barrier to hide it from the street, but it's active."

Vish glanced at the wall. "Is it safe to have a bar here?" he asked. "Wouldn't there be all kinds of chemicals in the area?"

"Sure." Poppy gestured with her chin at a multi-colored chemical hazard placard mounted on the bar. "It's not like they don't warn people. It's probably fine, as long as you don't lick the ground or anything."

A waiter came over, lithe and beautiful in a black collarless shirt, his dark hair swept off his face in a ponytail. "Your usual, Ms. Kang?"

"Please. Thanks, Alec." She turned to Vish. "What will you have?"

"Ah… The house red?"

The beautiful waiter smiled and nodded, as though he wholeheartedly approved of Vish's choice, then withdrew. As soon as they were alone, Vish cleared his throat. "I actually didn't come here to talk to Sparky about my book."

"Figured as much. What's on your mind?"

"I saw Sparky at Kelsey Kirkpatrick's birthday party. He said he'd gotten me into trouble, and he was sorry about it." Vish closed his eyes and tried to remember the exact words. "He said, '*She'll kill you if she can.*' I just want to know what he meant by that."

"Huh." Poppy raised her eyebrows until they disappeared under her heavy sheaf of bangs. She rested her elbow on the table and braced her chin in her hand. "That's enigmatic."

"That's what I thought," Vish said.

"Do you have any idea who 'she' is?"

Vish shook his head. "I thought he might be talking about my girlfriend, maybe. She dumped me immediately after the party, and I don't know why."

"Any reason she'd want to kill you?" Poppy asked.

"Not at all. Not even remotely." Vish exhaled. "It's all very confusing."

The waiter brought their drinks. A Manhattan for Poppy, four cherries. They drank in silence.

"This is Sparky's business, and I don't know how much I should tell you," Poppy said. She shrugged. "For that matter, I don't know the whole story. I imagine he'll find you at some point and explain things."

"Do you know if I'm in any danger?" Vish asked.

She smiled. "Don't worry about it," she said, and something about the way she said it, both kind and dismissive at once, made Vish feel better about the whole situation.

"Can you tell me anything about Sparky? Anything at all? What does he do? Why do people get so... weird about him?" Vish asked. "Lon Hartford said he runs things. What does he run?"

"It doesn't matter who he is," Poppy said. "If you need to know about him, he'll make sure you figure it out."

"You want to help me publish my book, and yet you won't tell me anything about who you—you and Sparky— really are?" Vish asked. "That doesn't seem very fair."

"Of course not. *Fair* doesn't factor into this." Another flash of dimples. "As I said earlier, it's a leap of faith. And it's entirely your decision. We'd be happy to work with you, but it's not going to crush us if you turn us down."

He could say yes. He could agree to work closely with Poppy, he could make the changes she'd suggested to his book, and maybe he'd find out more about Sparky in the process...

He shook his head. "Thank you for the offer, but no."

"Suit yourself." Poppy winked at him. She didn't seem upset by his decision, and Vish's chest relaxed. He hated confrontations, hated disappointing people, and somehow it seemed like a good idea not to annoy Poppy. "If you change your mind, you know where to find me."

"Why didn't you want to give me a ride?" Vish asked.

The smile faded. Poppy's brows drew together. "Sorry?"

"At the party in the hills, when you picked Sparky up after his car got wrecked. You shook your head at me when he offered me a ride."

"I did?" Poppy looked confused.

"You did. It seemed…." Vish thought a minute. "It seemed like it meant something."

"Well, it doesn't matter now, does it?" The smile returned, lighting up her beautiful face. "Sparky's odd. You've probably figured that out. I mean, I'm not going to say anything against him, because he's my boss and he's also a friend, sort of, but…" She shrugged. "Being around him tends to make life more complicated. I'm not saying I was trying to warn you, but things might've been simpler for you if you hadn't called Sparky."

"I met my girlfriend the day after that party," Vish said. "And she broke up with me right after I saw Sparky again."

"I know. You already mentioned that," Poppy said. "You're not very good at coming to the point, are you? You keep dancing around the subject, hoping I'll give you a different answer the next time you bring it up, but not wanting to ask any uncomfortable questions outright. I like you, Vish, but having a conversation with you is exhausting."

He wanted to explain that she had misread him, that he didn't know what uncomfortable questions to ask—something along the lines of "Did Troy only date me because of Sparky?" was close, but not quite right—but it didn't seem likely to help his case. "Did he ever find out who destroyed his car?"

157

"Of course he did," Poppy said. "Someone lost a role in a film and thought it was Sparky's fault. Which it may or may not have been—probably was, in fact—but you have to admit, that was a dumb way to deal with rejection."

"Did Sparky do anything about it?" Vish asked.

Poppy raised an eyebrow. "You really want to know?"

"He didn't... hurt whoever it was, did he?"

Poppy laughed. It seemed genuine, and Vish felt a rush of relief. "Sparky doesn't *hurt* people. I mean, the responsible party is probably never going to eat lunch in this town again, to invoke an old chestnut, but nobody got hurt, Vish. Not in any way that matters."

They finished their drinks. The waiter hovered nearby, but Poppy shook her head before he could ask if they wanted another. When the waiter brought the tab, Poppy laid a hand on Vish's wrist before he could pick it up.

"I'll put it on my expense report. We'll bill it to Sparky," she said.

"Thank you," Vish said.

"Anytime."

Vish hesitated. "Will you tell Sparky I want to speak with him?"

Poppy looked at him, her expression filled with a strange mixture of sympathy and amusement. "I'm pretty sure he already knows."

CHAPTER EIGHTEEN

"THERE'S SOMETHING LIVING under the building," Mariposa said.

Vish squatted beside her and squinted into the darkness of the crumbled corner. "I don't see anything," he said. "Is it what you thought you saw before?"

"It's still there. It's just a shadow, nothing else. But it moves." She placed a plastic bowl beside the orange safety cone marking the hole. The bowl was filled with what looked like mineral oil and a handful of leaves.

"What's that for?" Vish asked.

Mariposa shrugged. She seemed embarrassed. "Something I learned about from a girl at my job. She said it'd protect us."

He leaned down and examined the contents of the bowl. It smelled good, citrussy and astringent, reminiscent of Troy's perfume. "Do you mean like... magic?"

She scowled and shook her head. "It's not magic. And I'm not really doing it right. I'm supposed to use this little cauldron thing, but it was too expensive, even with my employee discount, so I figured the bowl would work okay. If there's something bad in the hole, this should keep it in there."

He stared at her for a moment. "Where do you work?" he asked.

"Luisa Botanica? It's near downtown, on Union," she said. "You know what a botanica is?"

"A plant store?"

She rolled her eyes. "Santeria supplies. Charms and candles and stuff. You know what Santeria is, right?"

"Sure. I mean, I don't know much about it, but I know what it is." Vish squinted into the hole. Whatever Mariposa was talking about, whatever she thought she saw, he couldn't see anything but darkness. "So you're into that kind of thing?"

"No. I don't know. I mean, it's just my job. But it's good to keep an open mind, you know?" She shrugged. "I figure it might help. Couldn't hurt, right?"

"Probably not," he said. He looked at the bowl. Santeria. Huh.

She threw him a sidelong glance. "I have to go to work now," she said. "If you want to see the place, you could come with me."

He considered. He had no plans, and it sounded like it could be interesting. "All right," he said.

She grinned at him. "Cool. Don't tell my mom, though. No boys in the car, right?"

Mariposa drove too fast, zipping down the freeway, weaving in and out of traffic. All the windows were down, and the radio blasted some relentlessly upbeat pop song. Vish was much too old for this kind of thing, but it was fun to lean back in the seat and watch the downtown skyline drawing closer. He liked downtown Los Angeles, the skimpy cluster of skyscrapers exploding up from the surrounding blocks of smaller historic buildings. Nice to have an excuse to visit.

Luisa Botanica took up the ground floor of a run-down building in a neighborhood that had seen better days. It wasn't any rattier than Venice, really, though it was a lot more crowded. Lots of activity, plenty of people on the street. Central American restaurants, discount stores with their signs in Spanish, doughnut shops, street vendors presiding over folding tables loaded with t-shirts and leather billfolds.

Inside, the botanica looked much like an ordinary drugstore. Fluorescent lights, dull white walls, peeling linoleum floors, rows of cheap metal shelves laden with goods. The merchandise, though, was decidedly different: Vish looked at racks of scented oils, at clay pots, at hammered metal crowns, at carved wooden figurines of voodoo deities. Religious texts in Spanish and English, seashells and bangles and beads and bottles. One entire aisle was devoted to candles, colorful ones housed in tall glass jars painted with vivid images of saints.

Mariposa nudged him in the side. "What do you think?"

"It's huge." Vish looked around. "I didn't know this sort of thing existed here, at least not on this scale."

"They're all over the city," Mariposa said. "You see them all the time if you're looking for them."

She beckoned him over to a shelf. "Look at this. Love charms. If you want to get your girlfriend back, you could use one of these."

Vish looked at a collection of small drawstring pouches, each one claiming to contain a spell to rekindle lost romance. Impossible to imagine winning Troy back this easily. Then again, she'd fallen for him almost at first sight, and when she left him, she'd acted like a spell had been broken…

He shook his head. Stupid to even indulge that kind of thinking.

"Who's your friend, Mariposa?" Vish turned to see a middle-aged woman glaring at him. Her expression was openly disapproving.

She looked elegant, yet severe. She wore a burgundy suit with a double row of gold buttons down the front. Dark hair anchored back into a tight chignon, gold-framed eyeglasses, chunky gold earrings shaped like rope knots. Her black stiletto pumps gave her a few inches on Vish.

"Hey, Isabella. This is my neighbor, Vish. I was just showing him the store. Isabella owns this place," Mariposa explained to him.

"I own the building," Isabella said. "Someone else owns the store and rents this space from me." When she looked at Vish, she didn't seem pleased with what she saw. "Vish, was it?"

"Yes, ma'am. Nice to meet you." He extended a hand. Isabella shook it. Firm grip. Her eyes never left his face.

"I wonder if I might borrow you for a moment, Vish. I'm rearranging some furniture in my office, and I could use an extra pair of strong hands."

"Of course. No problem."

"I need to punch in. You can get home from here okay, right?" Mariposa asked Vish. "Because otherwise I can drive you back on my lunch break, but I don't know if you're still going to be around then."

162

"I'll take the bus. Don't worry about it," Vish said.

Mariposa threw him a quick goodbye wave and headed for the counter by the front door. Vish followed Isabella out the emergency exit in back, which led into a short hallway. A nice old building, really, with small black-and-white tiles forming intricate geometric patterns on the floor and bronze pendant lamps shaped like fans drooping from the ceiling.

Isabella stopped in front of an office door. Gilt letters were painted on the frosted window: Isabella Madre, with a couple sentences of Spanish-language text beneath it. Vish managed to decipher a single word. *Notario*. "You're a law-yer?"

She nodded once, curtly, and unlocked the door. It opened into a waiting room that was only slightly roomier than an airplane lavatory. One folding chair, a wire display rack of brochures in Spanish, a potted palm wedged beside the door. Just beyond it was her private office. It was similarly tiny, with room for her desk, two client chairs, and a skinny metal filing cabinet. She had a framed diploma from Stanford Law and a calendar from the American Bar Association hanging on her wall.

Vish looked around. "What did you need me to move?" he asked.

"Nothing. I lied. Sit down, I want to talk to you." She closed the door and settled behind her desk, then pointed at one of the client chairs. Surprised, Vish obeyed.

"You're Mariposa's neighbor." It wasn't a question, but Vish found himself nodding.

"She lives in the apartment right next to mine," he said.

163

She stared at him over the rims of her glasses and said nothing. She'd be a demon in the courtroom, reducing witnesses to wrecked piles of nerves with little more than stern glares and well-timed silences. "You're much too old for her."

Vish gaped at her for a moment. "Oh," he said at last. "Oh. No. It's not like that. I'm just her neighbor. That's it."

Another hard stare. Vish wanted to fill the silence with more denials, but there was nothing more to be said—he *didn't* have improper designs on Mariposa, there was nothing to suggest he did, and it wasn't his problem if Isabella had misinterpreted the situation. Even still, he felt guilty and furtive, like he was trying to withhold secrets that she'd winnow out of him through icy stares and razor-sharp questions.

Isabella sat back in her chair. "She looked at you like she thinks you're more than a neighbor."

"I have no idea why she would," Vish said. "There's nothing between us."

"Then why are you hanging around her workplace?" she asked.

Well, good question. "I'd never heard of botanicas before Mariposa mentioned this place. I was curious." It was clear from her expression this wasn't enough of an answer, so Vish kept going. "She thinks something is living in the ground under our apartment complex, so she did… I don't know what you'd call it. I guess it's some kind of protection spell or something, though she says it's not magic."

Isabella nodded slowly. "And you? Do you think your building needs protection?"

"No, but…" Vish inhaled, shook his head. "No. I don't."

"But you need protection, don't you?" Isabella pointed a burgundy nail at the fading bruise on his forehead. "It looks like you found some trouble recently."

"I was mugged," he said.

"Uh-huh." Another long silence, and then she spoke: "I think you came here because you're searching for some help. Trouble has found you, and you don't understand why. Am I close?"

Vish didn't answer. He rose from his chair. "I'm sorry. I should get going."

"Just a moment." It was a command. "Wouldn't you like to know why?"

"I don't understand what you're talking about," Vish said.

"There's a mark on you," Isabella said. She shook her head. "That's not accurate, but it's a simple way to explain it. Someone marked you as someone of importance, and it's attracting the wrong people. I like Mariposa. She's a smart girl and a good kid. If she's hanging around you, she's in danger."

"A mark?"

"It's nothing visible. Nothing, really, that I can describe, either. It simply exists." She thought for a moment. "I sensed it as soon as you walked into my building. My eyes hurt a little just from looking at you, like the beginnings of a migraine headache." She smiled for the first time. "It's making me snappish. That's not your fault. I apologize."

"I'm not following this," Vish said.

"It's confusing, I know." Her expression softened. "I imagine this is already more of an explanation than Sparky has bothered to provide."

Vish stared at her. "Sparky?"

"You've been spending time with Sparky Mother. You have his mark on you, and it's getting you into trouble." She raised her eyebrows over the rims of her glasses. "You don't have to confirm or deny that. I don't need details."

"I've met Sparky Mother twice, very briefly. He didn't mark me."

The icy stare bored into him once more. "He gave you his phone number, didn't he? And you called him. And when you did, a connection was established between you. You became *important*." She almost seemed to be speaking to herself. "Someone else knew about that call, someone who wants what Sparky has."

"And what's that?"

"Hollywood." She smiled. "Isn't that what most people in this town want? Glamour and power and fame? Sparky's the key to all that." A shrug. "It often comes with a cost, of course. I imagine you've found that out for yourself already."

"How do you know all this?"

"Because Mariposa thinks something is living under your building." She glanced at him over the rims of her glasses. "Something crawled up from the earth and found you when you dialed Sparky's number. The ground shook, and everything changed."

It was weirdly hypnotic, listening to her talk. Nothing she said made much sense, and yet…

"How do you know Sparky?" he asked.

"We're very old friends." A smile, so cold it took his breath away.

"Can you tell me who he is?"

"No. I don't mean I won't. I mean quite literally I can't. I don't have the words to describe who or what he is. I'm not sure Sparky himself could tell you."

"You're talking about something supernatural, aren't you?" he asked. He didn't recognize his voice, which sounded odd and distant.

She didn't answer. She picked up a small notepad and scribbled something on it. She tore off the sheet and handed it to Vish. A few words in Spanish that meant nothing to him. "Give that to Mariposa and tell her I said to get it for you."

"What is it?" he asked.

"Protection. Something to hide the mark." She considered. "Did you ever have warts as a child?"

A confusing shift of topic. "Ah… once. On my knee," he said.

"How'd you treat it?" she asked.

"My mother was a doctor. She put some purple stuff on it and covered it with a bandage. After a couple of weeks it went away."

"Purple dye," Isabella said, nodding. "Iodine, probably, though what it really was doesn't matter. Simple food coloring would've worked just as well. Many parents did that, doctors or not. I'm sure some still do. Warts are a weak infection, and it often takes very little to make them go away. If you believe the dye is medicine that will make the wart disappear, it probably will."

Vish was about to respond, but the sound of the outer door to the hall closing startled him. Isabella glanced at her watch and frowned. "That's my next appointment. Give that to Mariposa. She'll know what to do."

She rose from her chair and moved toward the door. Relief that this strange and awkward encounter was over trumped Vish's desire to learn more about Isabella's connection to Sparky. He followed her out of her office.

A young couple, probably husband and wife, hovered anxiously in the tiny waiting area. Isabella shook their hands and spoke a few crisp words to them in Spanish, then led them into her office. She glanced back at Vish once, nodded at him, and closed the door.

Vish was tempted to just flee, walk out of the building and catch the next bus home, but he went back into the botanica anyway. Mariposa stood behind the cash register; he handed her the paper from Isabella. "Hey. She said you'd be able to get me this?"

Mariposa glanced down at Isabella's notes. "Yeah, sure." She pointed at a jewelry rack propped up on the counter. An array of bracelets dangled from it, colorful wooden beads strung on elastic string. "Pick your favorite color."

"Does it make any difference?" Vish asked.

Mariposa shrugged. "It's not like they do anything," she said. "They're just supposed to help people feel safe."

Vish picked out one with gray beads. It cost two dollars. Mariposa rang up the sale and handed it to him. "Here you go." She frowned. "Why'd Isabella want you to get one?"

"I couldn't really tell you." He slipped the bracelet around his wrist. With a wave goodbye to Mariposa, he left the store, feeling like an idiot.

CHAPTER NINETEEN

IT WAS THE newspaper delivery guy who spotted the dead man in the swimming pool and called 911 just after sunrise. Awakened by the noise of the ambulance at the front gate, Vish stepped out of his front door, looked down at the courtyard, and saw the body floating facedown in the water.

Mariposa came out of her apartment, clad in her night-clothes and her fuzzy pink slippers, and wordlessly joined him. They propped their elbows against the railing and watched the paramedics. One waded right into the water to check the drowned man's pulse. The dead man had blond hair, darkened by the water, and he wore shorts and a red shirt patterned with yellow hibiscus flowers.

"Wow," Mariposa said. "That's really awful. He doesn't live here, does he?"

Vish shook his head. His mouth was dry. He had to swallow before answering. That Hawaiian shirt… "I don't know. I can't tell who it is."

Police arrived immediately thereafter, two squad cars and a medical examiner in a white coroner's van. They photographed the body from all angles, then fished it out of the pool and laid it on a gurney. Vish and Mariposa remained standing at the second-floor railing, out of the way but observing the action. Mariposa seemed simply curious, neither upset nor ghoulishly intrigued.

A uniformed officer climbed up the stairs. "You live here?" she asked.

"I'm in this apartment right here, Mariposa's next door," Vish said. He looked at the officer. A familiar face, lovely and grim, wearing a short-sleeved uniform, legs bare and smooth beneath her shorts, on a clammy morning. Mirrored sunglasses on, even though the sun was still hidden behind the heavy marine layer. "Officer Guerrero?"

She looked startled, then slowly nodded. "You're the guy who got mugged at the beach last week. Sure. You had a strange name."

"Viswanathan. Well, Vish," he said.

"That's it. Either of you know who was in the pool?"

"I don't think he lives in the building. This place is pretty empty right now," Mariposa said.

Officer Guerrero turned her attention to Vish. Vish hesitated. "I don't know. Without seeing his face…"

Another nod. "You want to follow me?" she asked.

"Should I come too?" Mariposa asked.

Officer Guerrero shook her head. "Sit tight. I just want to check with Vish about something."

Vish trailed her down the stairs and over to the gurney, where the dead man's blanket-draped corpse lay. At a gesture from Guerrero, the medical examiner pulled back the blanket.

Death and submersion had turned the man's face gray and mottled. Vish stared at him for a moment. His eyes were open and sightless; rigor mortis had pulled the skin back from his purpling mouth, revealing long teeth and white-gray gums. Not young—in his forties maybe, with graying stubble across his chin.

"He look familiar?" Guerrero asked.

Vish hesitated. "I don't think so. But his clothes…"

"His clothes make you think he could be one of the guys who jumped you?" Officer Guerrero regarded him. Vish wished she didn't have the sunglasses on. If he could see her eyes, maybe he'd have a better idea what she was thinking. "You mentioned the Hawaiian shirts in your report."

"Yeah. I mean, I can't say either way. He's dressed like how they were dressed, but I don't recognize him specifically. But I didn't really get a chance to look at them closely." he said.

"If it's him, and if he wound up dead in your swimming pool, it seems like the sort of thing that'd have some connection to you."

"I agree. It does, though I have no idea what that connection could be."

She kept staring at him. At long last, she spoke. "You know, I talked to your girlfriend. Troy Van Whatever."

His heart stuttered a bit. "Oh?"

Officer Guerrero nodded. "Yeah. Stopped by her place. Nice girl. She served me tea and everything. She said she didn't know the guys you'd seen on the beach. Seemed pretty sincere. She said she didn't think you'd be involved in anything weird, either. Said you weren't the type." The corner of her mouth twitched. "Her roommate said you were square."

Vish didn't answer. At least Troy hadn't called him evil.

"I guess she's on a television show or something?"

"*Interstellar Boys*. I'm one of the writers."

"Never watched it. I think my brother's mentioned it." She smiled. "He's got a crush on one of the actresses. Probably your girlfriend."

She seemed to have unbent some. Maybe his connection to the glamour of Hollywood, tenuous as it was, made him seem respectable in her eyes. She considered.

"Okay," she said. "Until we ID this guy, I don't know how else you can help us. You think of anything important, don't be shy about giving us a call, okay?"

"Can I ask you something? Do you know if the guy just drowned, or if…?" He trailed off.

She took off the glasses at that. She had gorgeous eyes, huge and brown and limpid, like they belonged to a cartoon doe. "Or if something happened to him before he went in the pool?" she asked. "Got any reason to think that might be the case?"

"No. It just seems like a lot of police showed up here, if it was just a simple drowning."

She shook her head. "Call us," she said again. She nodded at the medical examiner, who pulled the blanket over the corpse, then walked over to the edge of the pool and stared down into the water. Vish returned to his apartment and drew the curtains so he couldn't see the activity outside. His phone was lying on the floor under his window. Huh. Not sure why it was there. He plugged it into the recharger in his bedroom and forgot about it.

The police stayed around into early afternoon. After they left, Silas stopped by. Vish heard him banging on each of his tenants' doors in turn, heard his muffled conversation with Mariposa and her mother, before he moved on to Vish's apartment.

"I suppose you heard about the body," Silas said.

"Yeah, I saw it. Pretty awful," Vish said.

Silas looked glum. Not surprising. A death in the building, even an accidental drowning, could bring trouble in the form of lawsuits or negligence charges or loss of income from renters reluctant to stay there any longer. "Just wanted everyone to know, it looks like someone's been squatting in apartment four. It's vacant, but cops noticed the lock looked funny, so I let them in, and they found some blankets and empty cans there. Could be whoever ended up in the pool."

Apartment four was on the ground level, the unit directly beneath his. "Kind of scary," Vish said.

"Yeah." Silas shrugged. "You're not leaving the gate unlocked or letting strangers into the complex, are you? The security fence exists for a reason, you know."

"I haven't. I haven't noticed anyone around who doesn't belong here," Vish said.

Silas looked mournfully over the railing at the pool. "Shouldn't have filled that damn thing," he said. "Knew it'd be more trouble than it was worth."

He moved on to the next unit. Vish closed the door behind him, then stood in his living room, lost in thought.

It was hard to know what was connected and what was coincidence. One of the surfers who jumped him on the beach

174

had maybe ended up dead in his pool. Maybe it'd been an accident, or maybe something more. And the guy had maybe been squatting in his apartment building before that. Maybe he'd been here to keep an eye on Vish.

A sudden, unwanted thought. His phone had been some-place he hadn't left it... Vish went into his bedroom, picked up his phone, and browsed through his history of recent calls. Since Troy had dumped him, he hadn't used it all that much. There shouldn't be anything new.

No. Apparently he'd made a call last night shortly after one. A local number, 310 area code.

He hadn't called anyone. He'd gone to bed early...

Fingers started to feel a little thick and numb. A landslide of dread slid over him. If someone else had made that call, had used his phone, had been in his apartment while he was asleep...

He scrolled through the features of his phone in search of clues. No recent text messages, either sent or received. He flipped through recent photos...

Vish's mouth went dry, because there was a photo of a dark room. His bedroom, to be specific. This was a photo of himself lying asleep in his bed, his comforter pulled up to his shoulders, his profile identifiable against his white pillowcase.

He almost dropped the phone. Someone broke into his apartment last night, used his phone to make a call, and took a picture of him while he was asleep.

And someone, maybe the same person, had ended up dead in the pool.

It was a violation, plain and simple. More, it was a message to him. Someone had expected him to find the photo; someone had wanted to provoke a response. Whoever snapped that photo would expect him to… what? Freak out? Hide? Go to the police?

He stared at the number someone had dialed from his phone. He didn't dare dial it himself, but maybe there was another way to figure out to whom it belonged. He went online and typed it into a search engine.

Success. The number came up in an online directory of payphones. Payphones were a dying breed, but there were still some out there, and someone had used his phone to place a call to one located at a restaurant called Mulgrew's in El Segundo. Mulgrew's, Vish discovered through a quick online search, was located close to the ocean on Vista Del Mar. Its website described it as a roadhouse; the menu offerings included fried clams and fish tacos and pitchers of beer.

He grabbed his keys and his wallet and headed out the door. Adrenaline kicked in; his knees felt shaky. The urge to move, to flee, was strong.

It wasn't any better being outside. The exposed, panicky feeling intensified. Being on the sidewalk was almost unbearable. Without quite understanding why he was doing this, he hopped on a bus. Heading south, heading toward El Segundo.

CHAPTER TWENTY

VISH EXPECTED SOMETHING seedy, but Mulgrew's was clean and comfortable. It was a ramshackle wooden structure with a wide, sprawling patio that faced the ocean. A row of shiny motorcycles were lined up in the crowded parking lot near the entrance; they might belong to customers, but they looked like props. Mulgrew's was a sanitized Hollywood version of a roadhouse, one geared more toward college kids and beachgoing tourists than legitimate tough characters.

He walked inside and was assailed by loud music. The interior was huge and airy, with exposed wooden beams plastered with bumper stickers. A glass case by the front register displayed t-shirts for sale. A waitress with a lot of curly blonde hair and a pink crop top edged past him on her way to the patio, balancing a tray of food on one shoulder. Baskets of onion rings and gigantic hamburgers. Vish's stomach growled. In all the excitement, he'd forgotten to eat today.

Vish looked around, uncertain. The payphone was located against the back wall, next to a sign pointing toward the restrooms. He could ask the waitress if she had worked last night, if she remembered anyone receiving a call at the payphone. Seemed like a long shot, but there wasn't much else he could do.

Except… Ah. At a booth in the far corner, sitting by himself, a bottle of beer on the table in front of him. Longish dark hair, an aristocratic nose, a black Hawaiian shirt. One of the surfers who attacked him on the beach, the ringleader. Vish was certain of it.

He should go. Duck out of the restaurant before he was spotted, call the police, tell them whatever he could.

He didn't. He navigated his way through the maze of tables and bodies and slid into the booth across from the surfer.

The surfer looked up. He was several years older than Vish, with a tanned face and very dark eyes. His hair was pulled off his face in a loose ponytail; dark wisps of hair fell in his eyes.

His expression didn't change at the sight of Vish. Then, finally, he smiled and settled back into the high wooden booth. "Balls," he said.

"Who are you?" Vish asked. He was pleased with how calm and confident he sounded. No hesitation, no nerves.

The surfer just stared at him for a moment. "Call me Tommy," he said at last. "I already know who you are."

"You attacked me on the beach the other day," Vish said. "I'd like to know why."

"Maybe I don't like you," the surfer—Tommy—replied. He took a swallow of his beer and smiled again.

"Yes, I got that," Vish said. "You broke into my apartment last night, didn't you?"

The smile morphed into a smirk. "Couldn't say. But it sounds like the sort of thing I'd do."

"Kind of stupid to use my phone, wasn't it? It led me right to you," Vish said.

"Yeah. Because that wasn't intentional at all," Tommy said. "I guess that was carelessness on my part. That sure wasn't me leaving you a trail of breadcrumbs so you could find your way here."

Vish felt a thrill of fear. "You couldn't have known I'd come. I could have called the police," he said. "I could have told them all about you."

"Probably should have," Tommy said. "Kind of dumb that you didn't, actually."

Vish glanced around. "We're in a public place," he said.

Tommy shrugged. "I got friends. Lots of friends. And people disappear in this city all the time." He locked eyes with Vish. "You're going to disappear, you know. Not today, probably, but just as soon as I get the word to go for it. Nobody's ever going to hear from you again." Another smile. "Maybe you should spend some time thinking about what I'm going to do to you. We'll have fun, you and me."

"Who's the dead guy in my pool?" Vish asked. "One of those friends of yours?"

A flicker of irritation crossed Tommy's face. He curled his upper lip. "Yeah. Joey. So you've got some friends too. So maybe Joey getting offed wasn't really your doing, but that doesn't mean we're not going to take it out on you."

"Who killed him?" Vish asked.

Tommy looked like he was about to reply. His glance shifted to just behind Vish, and he froze. "Well, hell," he said.

Vish turned and saw Poppy standing beside him. "Vish. I thought that was you. What a surprise."

Vish stared at her, unable to reconcile her presence in this setting. She was overdressed for the place in another tailored suit, this one in a deep violet. "Poppy," he said at last. "Why are you here?"

She held up a Styrofoam takeout container. "This place has the best loaded potato skins in the city. It's worth going out of my way."

She placed her free hand on his shoulder. "Come on. If you're done here, I'll give you a ride home."

Tommy glared at her. "We were talking," he said.

"Not anymore, Tom." The hand squeezed Vish's shoulder once, kind of hard. "Ready, Vish?" Her tone was brisk and cheerful.

Vish slid out of the booth. Poppy dropped her hand to his upper arm and closed it around it.

"See you soon, Vish," Tommy said. He gestured with his chin toward Poppy. "Maybe you too, sugar. Kind of interesting to think how your boss would react if you disappeared on him." He settled back, draping one long arm over the top of the booth, and smiled at her.

A corner of Poppy's mouth quirked up. "I wouldn't recommend trying to find out."

She half-marched Vish out of the restaurant. She didn't speak until they were out in the parking lot. "Really, Vish? That struck you as a good idea?" She shook her head. "And you seem so bright, too."

"He broke into my apartment last night," Vish said. "He took pictures of me with my phone."

"All of which was designed to scare you, or provoke you into a confrontation, and you took the bait." She stopped beside her sleek black car, all elegant lines and shiny detailing. "Hop in."

Vish obeyed. Poppy slipped behind the wheel. She handed her Styrofoam container to him. "Hang on to these," she said. Vish could smell bacon and onions and grease.

She slipped out of the parking lot and started heading north. "Why'd you go there?" she asked without looking at Vish. "You had to know that was dumber than hell."

"Because I'm tired of everyone knowing more about whatever is happening in my life than I do," he said. "Nobody answers my questions, and everyone seems to know what's going on, and I want it to stop."

"It's confusing, I know," she said. "That still doesn't give you carte blanche to be reckless."

"You told me I wasn't in any danger," he said.

"No. I told you not to worry about any danger, the implication being that I'd be around to bail you out in case you muddled into something you couldn't handle." Poppy smiled. "Hence my sudden need for loaded potato skins."

Vish stared at her. "You've been following me."

"No kidding." Poppy drove north on Vista Del Mar, heading up the coast. "And you're welcome."

"Did Sparky tell you to watch me?" he asked.

"Nope. This was on my own initiative. Mind you, he'd probably think it was a pretty swell idea. Turns out you're in desperate need of babysitting."

Vish stared at the passing scenery, at the oil refinery and the sewage treatment plant, great monolithic structures that rose up next to the ocean, monstrosities of shiny pipes and tall towers and vast metal tanks. Still keeping her hand on the steering wheel, Poppy pointed a finger at the refinery.

"Sparky loves El Segundo," she said. "All the refineries and crap. He goes crazy about that kind of thing. If it looks uninhabitable and apocalyptic, that's where he wants to live. I once had to talk him out of moving our offices to an oil platform off the coast. He tried to convince me the commute wouldn't be too bad."

"Who's Tommy?" Vish asked.

"Hired muscle. He works for someone who doesn't like Sparky very much." Poppy glanced at him. "Sparky's got a lot of enemies, and you're getting caught in the crossfire, which is totally his own damn fault. Sparky is maybe a little less concerned about it than he should be, which is why you've got me running interference for you."

"You know they found a dead body in the pool in my apartment complex this morning?" Vish asked. "Tommy called him Joey. He implied that someone got rid of him to protect me." When Poppy didn't answer, he swallowed hard and continued. "You didn't do anything to him, did you? You or Sparky or... anyone else?"

She snorted. "Wait for the medical report. It'll show you that no one did anything to anyone. The guy in your pool decided to dive in the shallow end in the middle of the night and, not surprisingly, broke his neck in the process. Autopsy'll show he had a bunch of illicit substances in his system."

"How do you know that?" Vish asked.

"I'm good at guessing. Just like I'm good at knowing what changes need to be made to a book to get it published, or to a screenplay to get it optioned."

They'd reached Marina Del Rey now, the usual tangle of docks and sloops and boats. "You're not going to tell me anything I want to know, are you?" Vish said.

She smiled. "Not directly, no. But surely you must be used to that by now." She turned onto Venice. "Try not to worry so much. Things will wrap up pretty soon. I can't say you'll get all the answers you're looking for, but…" She shrugged. "Odds are pretty good you'll get out of this alive, so there's that."

She pulled up in front of his apartment building, then reached over and took her food out of his hands. "I believe this is you."

"It is," Vish said. He glanced at her. "I haven't thanked you. I know I should."

"I get it. I won't feel snubbed if you're more frustrated than grateful." She smiled at him. "Take care of yourself, Vish. It's a scary world out there."

He climbed out of her car. She waved at him once and drove away.

CHAPTER TWENTY-ONE

THE GOOD THING about all the recent drama was how it distracted him from dwelling on his breakup with Troy. Still, Troy was always present in his thoughts, inextricably linked with everything that had happened since the explosion in the restaurant the night of Kelsey's party.

Vish paced his apartment, wound up. He didn't want to stay here, because it wasn't safe. He didn't want to go to the police, because nothing he could tell them made sense. He didn't want to go outside, because everyone seemed to have it in for him these days.

He touched the beaded bracelet. It didn't seem to be doing a good job of protecting him, because someone had broken into his apartment last night. Then again, they hadn't murdered him, or done any of the various other awful things they could have done, so maybe the bracelet was working. Or maybe murder was the next logical stage in their plans. Maybe they were still in the "scare the crap out of Vish" stage.

He went online, did another quick search for Sparky Mother. Still the same single lonely search result. He clicked on it and was transferred again to the AgentProwl message boards. He stared once more at the exchange between FutureStarr and DiegoXG.

Sparky Mother ruined my life.

It'd sure be nice if DiegoXG had provided a few specifics, but he'd never posted there again after that single enigmatic message. Vish stared at his laptop screen and chewed his lip.

He fed "DiegoXG" into a search engine. It spat back a handful of results. A smattering of social networking sites, plus his YouTube account, where he'd posted what looked like his acting reel.

DiegoXG. Diego Xavier Gonzales was barely out of his teens, with doe eyes and clear skin and a slight physique. His hair was cut too close to his head, which made his ears stick out. Adorable, but awkward. His reel consisted of clips from his appearances in student films.

And Sparky had ruined his life.

Diego had a personal website, too. He'd posted his résumé, riddled with typos, upon which he'd detailed his acting experience. Vish found himself piecing together a narrative of Diego's life and career. High school theater in Sacramento, including the role of Falstaff in *The Merry Wives of Windsor*, which was written by someone named Willaim Shakespere. No college, moved to Los Angeles to catch his big break, had yet to progress beyond unpaid local stuff. Nothing too impressive, not that Vish had any business feeling superior.

There was a phone number on his résumé, and an address. The address looked residential. Vish dialed the number.

Disconnected. A tinny operator's voice informed him it was no longer in service.

Well. What now? He could go to the address and try to talk to Diego in person. Diego might think he was a lunatic for tracking him down this way. Or he might not—Sparky was an odd bird, and Diego might have a good story about his dealings with him. Vish thought for a moment, then headed for the bus stop.

Diego's address fell within the border of Koreatown, the sprawling area that started downtown and spread all the way west to the Miracle Mile. He lived in an apartment complex on Sixth, just off of Vermont, in a brownstone building with a crumbling archway over the front entrance.

According to his résumé, Diego lived in apartment 414. He must be a trusting sort; that was a lot of dangerous personal information to put out on the internet. The call box out front didn't work, but the main door was unlocked, so Vish just took the stairs up to the fourth floor. The carpet was threadbare, and the corridor smelled like stale beer and wet dogs.

Vish knocked on Diego's door. After a long pause, long enough to make Vish consider slipping a note under the door and leaving, the door opened a crack. A young blonde woman in a tank top peeked out at him from under the chain lock. "What?"

"I'm sorry for disturbing you. I'm looking for Diego Gonzales?"

The woman frowned. She shook her head. "He's not... He isn't here. What do you want with him?"

"It's sort of a long story," Vish said. "I think we might have mutual friends. I wanted to ask him about someone." The woman continued to stare at him, so Vish tried again. "Do you know if he'll be back soon?"

"Who's your friend?" she asked.

"Sparky Mother?"

She stared at him for a moment longer, then said, "Just a second." The door closed. Vish heard her fumbling to unhook the chain lock, then the door opened again. "You can come in if you want," she said.

Vish entered and glanced around the apartment. A tiny white-walled living room with a refrigerator standing in the corner beside a ratty red futon sofa, a microwave and coffee maker on top of an end table, a cardboard box filled with cups of instant soup and boxes of granola bars beneath it.. A pasteboard bookcase sagging under the weight of stacks of plays and sheet music, unframed movie posters taped directly to the walls.

"My name is Vish," he said. "I'm sorry for disturbing you like this."

"I'm Gina," she said. She was small-boned and birdlike, with a lot of pale curly hair and delicate features. The bones of her shoulders protruded like aborted wings from either side of her tank top straps. White leggings made her legs look skeletal. "Diego was my roommate."

"He doesn't live here anymore?"

She shrugged. "Good question. I don't know. Thing is, I haven't seen him in a month. So maybe he moved out without telling me and left all his crap behind, or…" She spread her hands. "Maybe something happened to him. I don't know."

"Wow," Vish said. "Is anybody looking for him?"

"His parents came down from Sacramento. I called them when he didn't come home for a couple of nights. I didn't know what else to do. They filed a missing persons report." She rolled her shoulders back, like she was stretching a cramped muscle. "They're not real close to him."

"What do you think happened to him?" Vish asked. "I mean, are there signs of…" He was about to say "foul play," but that sounded too dramatic. "…anything going wrong?"

She exhaled. "Don't know. His bank statement says he's got a couple hundred in checking still. If he left town for some reason, you'd think he'd take that. He left a bunch of clothes and stuff here, but he kept his room kind of messy, so it's hard to know if anything's gone. Took his car, his phone, his wallet." She shrugged. "Your guess."

"You didn't know him that well?"

"Met him in my acting class. I needed a roommate, he seemed like a nice guy. He was a nice guy. Is a nice guy, I hope. I don't know what to think." She looked at Vish. "You said you know him through Sparky Mother?"

"I don't know him at all," Vish said. "He posted on a message board for actors. He said Sparky Mother ruined his life. I had a chance to work with Sparky, but I haven't been able to find out anything about him, so… I was just curious."

Gina stared at him. "Huh," she said finally. "Well, you wasted a trip. Even if Diego was here, I don't think he could tell you anything useful."

She flopped down on the futon and folded her skinny legs up beneath her. She didn't offer a seat to Vish, so he remained standing, feeling like he was taking up too much space in the tiny room. "Diego was up for a guest spot on a TV show. I don't even know how close he was, but Diego said

188

he had a good feeling about the audition. And he met this guy there, Sparky Mother, who was representing some other actor, and the other actor got the role, even though Diego didn't think he was any good. He thinks this Sparky person bullied the casting director into not casting him." She gave Vish a lopsided smile. "Ergo, Sparky Mother ruined his life."

Whatever explanation Vish had expected, this wasn't it. This was such a pallid little nothing of a tale, all about an actor's fragile ego and his need to blame setbacks on outside sources. "Oh," he said.

"Yeah. Oh." She smiled. "So, I mean, this Sparky guy could be legit or bad news, but I don't think Diego would have much to say either way. I wouldn't even have remembered this, except it's kind of a funny name. Stuck with me, I guess."

Vish cleared his throat. "You don't remember what TV show it was, do you?"

"It's on cable. I've only seen it a couple times, and it's really crappy. *Interstellar Boys?*"

At this point, he didn't know why he was surprised. "Well. I'm really sorry I bothered you. I hope Diego turns up safe."

"Thanks." Gina looked glum. "You know anyone looking for an apartment? I can't keep paying rent on this whole place."

It took some doing to convince Gina he wasn't interested in moving into Diego's abandoned room. She badgered him into taking a fast tour of the place before he managed to say his goodbyes and leave.

He was hungry. Unwilling to face the bus to the beach without food, he popped into a Korean coffee shop on the ground floor of a multistory office building. The place was clean and tiny, with circular acrylic tables in gumdrop colors and shiny chrome stools. The menu, which hung on a lighted sign above the register, was entirely in Korean, but there were helpful photos beside each item. Coffee and tea, cheesecake and pastries and gelato.

The pretty woman behind the counter didn't speak English, but she smiled and nodded when he asked for a cup of coffee and pointed to a croissant in the display case. He perched on a child-sized stool at one of the little tables and drank his coffee.

Could Diego's disappearance be linked to Sparky? Or even to Troy? There was that good-natured actress on *Interstellar Boys*, the guest star who'd gone missing after she'd had drinks with Troy and him. Carlotta. It was a coincidence, probably, and probably whatever had happened to Diego was unrelated as well, but…

Vish finished his croissant. He was just considering leaving when someone plopped down onto the stool across from him. It was Sparky.

Sparky wore another expensive suit, dove-gray with a lilac-colored shirt beneath it, and it fit him like it'd been meticulously tailored to his precise measurements. Apart from that, he looked like hell. His nose was rimmed in red; his dark blue eyes were bloodshot. He gave Vish a lopsided smile and held up a hand before he could speak. "We'll talk. I promise. I need to eat first."

190

As if on cue, the woman who'd taken Vish's order placed two enormous white bowls on their table. Flat noodles and cabbage in a bright orange broth, topped with gigantic red prawns. Didn't look like anything on the menu above the counter. Sparky flashed his teeth and said something in what seemed to be fluent Korean to her; she smiled and said something back.

Sparky gestured to the soup. "Hot food," he said to Vish. "You look like you need it. So do I." He wiped at his nose with a handkerchief. "I've been trying to get over this blasted sickness."

"It's been going around," Vish said.

"No kidding. And it's all your girlfriend's fault." At Vish's confused look, Sparky rolled his eyes and continued. "Kelsey Kirkpatrick's party. She trailed me into the little boys' room and smashed some itty-bitty bottle of foul nastiness on me. Whatever was in it, it put me out of commission for a while."

The necklace he'd bought for Troy, with the bottle pendant, the one that had disappeared during the party. "Troy caused the explosion?"

Sparky dug into his soup. "Not her, *per se.* It's complicated."

"Explain," Vish said. Sparky seemed to be eating his soup with gusto, so Vish sampled his. It was delicious—sour and salty and comforting, with a rich, flavorful broth with all manner of tasty bits floating in it.

Sparky sighed. "Okay, so there's someone out to get me. Multiple parties, actually, but that's what happens when you have a lot of power like me, even though I'm kind of an awesome guy. And I'm only really talking about one particular party here."

"The person who wrecked your car," Vish said.

Sparky shook his head. "Nope. That was small potatoes. Piddling kid stuff, already dealt with. Like I said, I've got enemies."

"Troy?"

"I've never met Troy. That thing that attacked me at Kelsey's party, that thing you were canoodling with for a month, that wasn't Troy. That was something that was just borrowing her for a bit."

Vish just stared at him. Sparky slurped down more of his soup, then shrugged. "Okay, I'll spill. From the beginning. I knew someone was after me, and I knew who it was, but I needed to lure him into the open. Not that he could do anything to me, not really, and he knew that, but he was being pretty damned irritating. So at Maryanne's party, I gave you a phone number. A phone number that, for a while, made you the most important person in Los Angeles. And my friend was monitoring that number, and as soon as you called me, he came after you."

"The earthquake," Vish said. "The blackout. Someone hit me over the head."

"Is that how he found you? Sounds about right. Anyway, it's not useful to think in terms of *someone*. Something. Something hijacked you then, and stayed with you until your paths crossed with another person. Someone this thing could then hijack, who could stay in your life and keep an eye on you until you led it to me."

"Troy," Vish said.

Sparky nodded. "Troy. And this thing stuck around inside Troy, until it had a chance to attack me at Kelsey's party. At which point it left, and Troy—the real Troy—found herself saddled with a boyfriend she didn't especially want and wasn't quite sure why she was with in the first place."

"So nothing about my relationship with Troy was real?" Vish asked. "From the start?"

Sparky stared at him. "No, Vish," he said. "The knockout television star fell head over heels for some caterer of her own accord."

"Fuck you," Vish said. He'd never said that to anyone before, but it popped out on its own. Felt pretty good.

"Careful," Sparky said. He raised an eyebrow, and though his amiable expression didn't change, Vish knew there was danger here somewhere.

He inhaled. He still felt shaky with anger, but calmer. "If it wasn't Troy, than who was it?"

"Just a rival," Sparky said. "Something very old, something that lives deep in the earth and doesn't like how much control I have over this town. After I cut out a niche for myself in Hollywood, it decided it wanted in on that sweet action." He looked around the café. "I mean, for crying out loud, why would anyone come to Los Angeles if they weren't going to be in the industry? It's not like this place has much else to recommend it."

"And your rival?" Vish asked.

"Was jealous about how much power I had. He wanted to take my place, but I'm too much for him to deal with. I had

193

that territory covered, and there was nothing he could do about it. So he took over the beaches. Surf culture, crap like that. But he still wants what I have, so he keeps nipping at my ankles every chance he can find."

"'He'?" Vish asked. "Is your rival an 'it' or a 'he'?"

"Either works. 'It' is more accurate."

Vish stared at him for a while. "What is he—or it— really?" he asked.

"To the best of my knowledge, he's a big-ass earthworm." Sparky grinned. "I'm not being facetious. I've only seen him once in his natural guise, or what I figure is his natural guise, but he's this enormous wormlike thing. Ridges and all. Kind of cool. Every time he comes to the surface, the earth shakes."

"My neighbor says there's something living in the earth under my apartment. Is that…?"

"One of his minions, my guess. He probably sent something to keep an eye on you whenever Troy wasn't around."

The grubs under his sink. "I was in love with… a giant worm?"

"Yeah, pretty much." Sparky winked. "Love is blind, right?"

Vish fell silent. Sparky thought for a minute. "He's been killing actors," he said at last. "Or his surfer cronies have, most likely. Under-the-radar actors, probably writers too, maybe musicians or whatever, fringe people in the industry. Los Angeles' single greatest renewable resource."

"Why?" Vish asked.

"To annoy me. It hits me at my power base. So he put together this band of thrill killers, his little coterie of psychotic surfer types, and fueled their baser needs. Sicced them on all those kids who come out here to be famous." Sparky tilted his head to the side, considering. "So it looks bad for me. I figure it's my responsibility to stop him."

He glanced down at the table, then began to snicker. "Yeah, that'll help," he said. "Going to try smearing yourself with chicken blood and dancing naked in the moonlight next?"

Vish glanced down at the beaded bracelet on his wrist, the object of Sparky's mirth. His cheeks felt hot. "It's not like wearing it could hurt," he said. He sounded defensive and petulant.

"That's what you think." Sparky held out his hand. "Don't fool around with things you don't understand."

Vish hesitated, then slipped off the bracelet and passed it to Sparky. Sparky turned it over and examined it. He snorted. "Well, never doubt the power of suggestion, I guess," he said.

"The woman who gave it to me was a friend of yours," Vish said. "Isabella Madre."

Sparky raised an eyebrow. He stuffed the bracelet in the pocket of his suit coat. "You do get around, don't you?" he said. "Isabella. Outstanding. I'm surprised she helped you. You're not her responsibility."

"What does that mean?" Vish asked.

Sparky shrugged. "Division of the city. I handle the entertainment industry, so I'm responsible for you, more or less. Troy—we're still calling him Troy, remember, but that's just shorthand—has the beaches. Isabella's got the tired and poor, the huddled masses yearning to breathe free."

"Immigrants?"

"Yep. She picked that for herself. She might be the only soul in the city who genuinely doesn't give a crap about Hollywood." He pursed his lips in thought. "Could be she has a soft spot for you. Your parents weren't born here, right? Maybe that was close enough to count."

"Is she related to you?" Vish asked. "Madre, Mother?"

"'Mother' is a very common last name," Sparky replied stiffly and, to the best of Vish's knowledge, wholly inaccurately. "Does it seem like we're related?"

Vish shrugged. "It could be. You don't look entirely unlike her."

Sparky didn't say anything. He stared at Vish, a self-amused smirk dancing on his lips, and finally Vish made the connection. "This isn't what you look like either, is it?"

"Not even close," Sparky said.

"Are you a giant worm, too?"

"I assure you, no. I'm just as good-looking in my natural form." Sparky leaned forward over the tiny table. "We're not related, Isabella and Troy and I, but you can think of us as siblings, if you like. There's a few more of us in the city, too."

"Where'd you all come from?" Vish asked.

"None of your business." Sparky smiled. "Your role in this is almost wrapped up."

"Almost?"

"Just one more thing I need you to do for me."

It occurred to Vish far too late that something was wrong inside him. A numbness in his throat, a burning in his stomach. The soup...

"When you look back on this day, you'll realize giving me this wasn't your finest moment." Sparky held up the bracelet. "Did it never occur to you that Isabella gave you this to protect you from *me*?"

Vish stared at him. "What have you done?" he asked.

"Really, Vish, have recent events suggested I'm someone you should trust?"

Vish couldn't think of anything to say. Sparky looked nonchalant. "The Troy-creature is still out there, you know, now that he's left your ersatz girlfriend." He shrugged. "He used you to draw me out and attack me, now I'm using you to do the same. It seems appropriate."

He leaned across the table and patted Vish lightly on the cheek. "See you around," he said, and strolled out of the coffee shop.

Vish rose. His chrome stool scraped across the tile floor. At the table next to his, a willowy young Korean woman in dark jeans and a green fur jacket looked up from her phone and scowled at him. He didn't know what she could see in his face, but she quickly looked away.

The restroom was in the back of the restaurant, down the short hallway that led to the kitchen. It was unlocked and unoccupied, thankfully. Vish locked the door behind him and forced himself to throw up, as quietly as he could. His esophagus felt like it had been scorched.

He was dumb. Goddamn, he was dumb. Trusting Sparky, listening to Sparky, giving his bracelet to Sparky... His vision blurred. Cold pools of sweat collected on his stomach and in the small of his back; his legs shook and his face felt hot.

Awesome.

He guzzled tap water from his cupped hands, then sponged down his face and his back and chest with wet paper towels. He stared at himself in the mirror. He gripped the sides of the sink to keep himself on his feet. He looked okay. A little manic, maybe. His pupils overwhelmed his irises.

A knock on the door. "Hey, man, everything okay in there?"

"Sorry," Vish said. "Just a minute." He dried his hands and opened the door.

A young man stared at him. Korean, early twenties, jeans and Converse and a green hoodie. "Are you all right? You ran in here pretty fast."

"I'm fine. Sorry. Getting over the flu," Vish said. "Sorry."

"Sit down." The man led him to a bench in the hallway. "You look like you're about to pass out."

Vish sank down onto the bench and leaned his back against the cold concrete wall. He closed his eyes.

"As soon as the guy you were with left, you looked really freaked out. I thought he'd said something to upset you."

"He did," Vish said. "But it's okay."

He took a deep breath and composed himself. He got to his feet. "I should go."

"I'll walk you to your car," the young man said. He looked like a slightly old college kid, maybe a grad student at UCLA or USC.

Vish shook his head. "I took the bus."

The man hesitated. "Do you need a doctor? I could call an ambulance. I don't think you should go on the bus."

"Thank you. I'll be fine," Vish said. "I just need to get home."

"Where's home? I'll drive you."

"I'm at the beach. Venice," Vish said. "Thank you, but don't bother. It's too far away."

The young man took his arm and guided him toward the back exit. "I'm parked in the back lot. It's no big deal. I have stuff I can do in Santa Monica anyway."

The offer seemed to be in earnest, and Vish was in no shape to turn it down. "Okay. Thank you," he said.

"No problem." The young man guided him over to his car. "I'm Philip, by the way."

"Vish."

"Nice to meet you, Vish. Sorry, my car's kind of a mess. Is it faster on the 10 this time of day, or should I just take Wilshire?"

"I couldn't say," Vish said. He shifted an empty water bottle and a stack of thick medical textbooks from the passenger seat to the floor, then settled in the car and rested his head against the back of the seat. It felt good to close his eyes. He wanted to explain that he didn't have a car and thus didn't know much about the flow of traffic on the freeways at various times of the day, but that would take more energy than he had available, so he kept quiet.

"I still think we should go to a hospital," Philip said. He turned onto Wilshire and headed west. "You seem kind of out of it."

"No, really," Vish said. "It's not as bad as it seems. I just need to get some rest."

Philip drove in silence for a while. Then: "Why'd he poison you?"

Vish opened his eyes. "I'm sorry?"

"You know who I'm talking about," Philip said. He didn't take his eyes off the road. "Sparky. I thought he was protecting you."

Vish stared. "Who are you?" he asked.

Philip smiled. "Oh come on, Vish," he said. "After all the time we spent together, don't you recognize me?"

Vish straightened up in the seat. His hand closed around the passenger door handle.

"Hello, Troy," he said.

CHAPTER TWENTY-TWO

"Troy." Philip smiled. "That's not really my name, you know." He gestured at the door handle. "Stay put. You're in no shape to be on your own right now."

"What do you want?" Vish asked.

"For starters, I'm interested in finding out why Sparky turned on you. And here I thought you two were close."

Vish laughed. It sounded high-pitched and demented, and it scared the hell out of him. "I really couldn't tell you," he said.

"You'll tell me," Philip—Troy—said. "You'll tell me everything, starting with why you're so important to Sparky."

"But I'm not," Vish said. "I haven't ever been. I've been a decoy." It stank to say it out loud like that. "He was trying to lure you out, so he gave me his phone number, knowing you'd be on to me as soon as I called him. And now that I'm not any use to him, I guess he decided to get rid of me."

Philip looked at him. "Huh," he said at last.

They drove in silence. Vish was okay with that. It was difficult to concentrate, what with the way his head kept swimming. He kept his hand on the door handle, and at every red light, he considered swinging it open. He'd leap to the curb, make a break for it, find a cop or anyone who could help him.

No. Bad plan. He was sick and weak. He'd conserve his energy and choose the right moment to make his move, whatever that might turn out to be.

He looked at Philip. "Why'd you choose Troy?" he asked. "Why her?"

"Chance. I made a fast decision when you first encountered her," Philip said. "The original plan was just to stick with you, but I figured Sparky would never show his face if he knew you were..." He stopped and appeared to mull over the correct way to phrase it.

"Possessed?"

"Possessed, or compromised, or hijacked, or however you want to describe it. Anyway, I thought it'd be more interesting for everyone concerned if I used Troy. I hope you're not complaining, because you were awfully happy with her. With me, I should say."

"You seemed to know me pretty well," Vish said. "You knew exactly how to manipulate me."

"How to make you fall in love with me, you mean?" Philip smiled. "I'm a quick study." He reached out and touched Vish's jawline. Vish flinched away. It was a gesture Troy would have made, before she woke the morning after Kelsey's party to discover some... creature... had been occupying her body for the past month.

No wonder she'd thought Vish was evil.

The scenery along Wilshire flew by. Miracle Mile blended into Beverly Hills, which blended into Westwood, then Brentwood and Santa Monica, and finally Vish could see the ocean. Philip headed north on the Pacific Coast Highway, past

Pacific Palisades, and from there Vish lost track of where they were. This was one of those areas people without cars couldn't easily reach, out where the Santa Monica Mountains ran into the sea.

Philip turned onto a side street and drove up into the hills, then pulled onto the shoulder and parked. They were at the top of a bluff, a couple hundred feet above the PCH and the sandy beach just beyond it. "Get out," he said. Vish tried to obey, but realized he didn't have enough strength in his hands to get the door open. His chest and stomach burned when he tried to move.

He tried again. Damn it, if he couldn't walk, he couldn't escape.

Philip huffed out an impatient sigh, then stormed around to the passenger side and opened the door. He grabbed Vish by the arm and yanked him out. Vish tumbled to the gravel and landed on his shoulder. Didn't hurt much. He wasn't feeling much of anything, which was surely cause for alarm.

Philip kicked him in the chest once, hard. Okay, he felt that.

"Get up," Philip said. "Move it, or I'll really hurt you."

Vish stared up at the sky, white from the marine layer. This was one of the things he'd liked most about this city when he first moved here, how the beaches looked so beautiful and desolate sometimes, apocalyptic in their wide emptiness, the ocean and sky so obscured by that strange white haze that it was impossible to see where one ended and the other began.

Another kick to his ribs yanked him out of his thoughts. Philip reached down and grabbed the back of his shirt and hauled him to his feet.

"We're going down the cliff," Philip said. He gestured at a dirt trail leading down through the rocks and dry grasses. "If you can't walk on your own, I'll drag you."

"I can walk," Vish said. Might even be true. In any case, hiking to the PCH wasn't a bad idea. Plenty of traffic, plenty of people. Whatever Philip was going to do to him, he'd be hard-pressed to try it in such a public spot.

Philip gave him a small shove. Vish headed down the trail. It was steep and slippery with loose rocks and dirt, but he could manage it. He moved as quickly as he could. Philip was right behind him, within tackling distance, but maybe he wouldn't dare to attack him with so many potential witnesses around.

He'd never get a better chance than this. Vish picked up the pace. Legs felt unsteady, and he was dangerously close to falling on his ass, but it felt better being in motion. He'd make it to the highway and flag down a motorist. He'd be saved.

He heard Philip shout something, and then a body slammed into him from behind. Vish tumbled forward; someone grabbed his hair and yanked him upright. Vish turned his head and found himself looking at a familiar face. Not Philip. Tommy.

"Going somewhere?" Tommy asked.

Philip slid down the bluff to join them. "Sparky poisoned him. He's dying. We need to find out what he knows first."

"My pleasure," Tommy said.

Tommy had come from nowhere, materializing out of the ether. He hadn't been at the top of the bluff when Vish and Philip had arrived, and yet he'd attacked Vish from behind. Even as Vish stared at him, though, the mystery cleared up. A head of shaggy fair hair poked out of the side of the bluff, and then another surfer joined their motley little group. "Hey, you got him, huh?"

He'd emerged from a cave in the side of the hill, a small hole, the entrance obscured by scraggly bushes and an outcropping of rock. Tommy marched Vish through the opening and shoved him to the ground. One more surfer was inside, seated cross-legged on the sandy floor. Four against one. Not great odds.

Vish squinted in the darkness at his surroundings and saw craggy rocks and damp sand. Philip crouched in front of him. "Can you move?" he asked.

Vish sat up. Slowly, because everything swam and spun and shifted at every motion. Standing was beyond him, so he leaned his back against the cave wall. The cold dampness seeped through his shirt.

Philip leaned forward and examined him. "You're dying," he said. "But before you do, you're going to tell me all you know about Sparky."

Vish tried to laugh, but it hurt his chest. "Already done," he said. His voice was thin and wobbly, no power behind his words. "There's nothing more to say."

He took a deep, painful breath. "Sparky wanted to use me to figure out what you're up to. That's all."

"Did he, now?" Philip sat back on his heels and examined him. "Tommy, why don't you show Vish what we're up to?"

Tommy grabbed Vish by his upper arms and hauled him to his feet. "This way," he said. Vish found himself half-pushed and half-dragged down a short, sandy tunnel at the back of the cave.

Before he could see anything, the stench hit him first, a combination of decay and something worse, and Vish knew without having ever smelled this particular odor before that the chamber was filled with corpses.

Philip lit a match, a spark of bright light in the darkness, and touched it to a torch jammed into the sand. Glittering lights dazzled Vish's eyes. Thousands of sparkly polished stones set into the cavern walls formed intricate mosaics, violent images of great beasts and gigantic figures flickering in the firelight, scenes of some long-forgotten mythology, about which he'd never know more than what could be gleaned from these fragmented glimpses. There were answers here, clues to the true nature of Troy and Sparky and Isabella, and Vish wished he'd never seen any of it.

And then there were the bodies, close to two dozen of them, all in a pile, limbs tangled, sprawled in a careless heap on the sandy floor. Some recently killed, some nothing more than browning bones draped in rags and scraps of rotting flesh. The missing actors, the ones who'd disappeared, this was where they'd ended up. This was what Philip—Troy, or whoever he really was—had done to spur Sparky into action. Maybe Diego Xavier Gonzales was here, or maybe he'd simply cut his losses and left town after deciding stardom wasn't in his cards. Maybe Carlotta was here, too, that cheerful and friendly actress who'd been so happy about her bit part on *Interstellar Boys*. Collateral damage in some tiff between Sparky and one of his many enemies.

"Why?" he asked. He wanted to say more than that, but there was no power in him.

Philip smiled, cold and fleeting. "Which answer would be better?" he asked. "That I enjoyed it, or that I didn't care?"

He gestured with his chin toward the surfers. "Their doing, most of it," he said. "They had the enthusiasm. I gave them free reign and told them I could protect them if they got caught."

He nodded at Tommy. "Care to finish what you started?"

They were on Vish, kicking and grabbing and groping and tearing, and Vish could do little more than lie there and take it. He tried to crawl away or, failing that, protect himself as best he could, but he couldn't move, couldn't coordinate his muscles and get his brain to send the right messages to his body.

Then, as suddenly as it began, it stopped. The blows ceased. The surfers froze. Vish raised his head.

"Oh, hey." Sparky stood in the entrance to the cavern. "Looks like I finally found you guys." He nodded at Vish. "Thanks, Vish. How are you holding up?"

Vish couldn't answer. He concentrated on taking normal breaths. His chest hurt in an ominous way.

Sparky didn't seem to expect an answer from him. He turned his attention to Philip. "You seemed hell-bent on luring me out of my comfort zone. So here I am."

"This isn't your territory, Sparky," Philip said. "Coming here was a bad idea."

Sparky just smiled. He glanced at the pile of corpses in mild interest, then turned to look at Tommy and the surfers. He didn't move, or do or say anything. A smile tugged at the corners of his lips.

A rush of air, like an errant gust of wind, and then the surfers burst into flames.

CHAPTER TWENTY-THREE

VISH HAD NO clue what had happened. The surfers had been standing there, staring at Sparky, and Sparky hadn't moved, but now they were enveloped in blue-white fire, supernova-bright. Vish was only a couple feet away; he instinctively recoiled back, but the flames radiated no heat. The cavern seemed colder now, in fact, much colder.

Chaos broke out, shrieks and shouts as the surfers flung themselves to the sandy floor and rolled around in an attempt to extinguish the flames. Skin reddened and blistered and charred. After one glance, Vish couldn't look at them.

Philip's eyes rolled back in his head, and he crumpled to the sand. The ground shifted and lurched. Rocks and chunks of earth rained down from the top of the cave.

"What's happening?" Vish asked Sparky. He tried to yell, but he couldn't get enough air, and his words, thin and breathless, got lost somewhere in the rumble of the earth and the shrieks of the dying surfers.

"This'll be good," Sparky yelled back, his voice carrying over the commotion. "He's reverting to his true form. I'm going to follow suit." He shot Vish a jaunty thumbs-up. "Keep your eyes shut. If you see what I look like, you won't leave here alive."

A roar and a screech, and then the back wall of the cave exploded, turning the mosaics into a glittery shower of multicolored tiles. An avalanche of dirt and sand poured down over Vish.

Vish shut his eyes so tightly his temples ached from the strain. The cave was collapsing, and bad things were happening, and he needed to get out of there. Sightless, he crawled in the direction of the exit. He bumped into a body slumped on the ground. Must be Philip. He was warm and breathing, though unconscious.

Blue-white light penetrated through Vish's shut eyelids. A high-pitched hum soared above the terrible rumble and reverberated through his chest. The surfers had long since stopped making any noise at all; a stench of charred meat hung heavy in the air, overpowering the older, fouler smell of decomposition.

Vish stood up, eyes still screwed shut. Pain erupted all over his body in little volcanic bursts, but he was alive and determined to stay that way. He groped around for Philip, then grabbed him under the armpits and dragged him out of the cave. He didn't dare open his eyes until he heard the traffic noises of the PCH, felt the clammy ocean air against his face.

He dragged Philip down the remainder of the bluff to the side of the highway. He glanced back at the opening of the cave. White smoke streamed out of the opening in great clouds.

Vish couldn't guess what was going on in the battle between Sparky and the Troy/Philip creature, and he didn't want to know. It was something bigger than him, and it involved him only in a tangential way, and his part was over.

Philip opened his eyes. He looked at the highway, at the smoke billowing out of the cave, at Vish. He got to his feet and stared at Vish in confusion and dawning horror.

"I took you... I don't know why... I didn't..." He seemed a heartbeat away from dissolving into hysterics. Vish didn't have the energy for that.

"It wasn't you," he said. "Something took over your body for a bit. It's gone now." He pointed at the cave. "It's in there. I think that's where it lives."

Philip looked at him in incomprehension, eyes wide. From somewhere in the distance, further north on the PCH, Vish heard a siren.

He thought fast. "We met in Koreatown, and you offered to give me a ride back to Venice. We decided to drive up to this beach to go hiking. And those surfers attacked us and dragged us into the cave with all those bodies, and somehow a fire broke out. That's all we know."

Philip stared at him. He shook his head. "I didn't..."

"For the police," Vish said. "If the police ask us about it, that's what we have to tell them, because the truth doesn't make sense."

After a moment, Philip nodded, slowly. "They attacked us and took us to the cave," he said.

"Right," Vish replied. "Are you okay with that?"

Philip nodded. He looked like he was about to cry. Vish could understand that. He probably looked the same.

Standing took too much energy. Vish sat down on the cement barrier diving the bluff from the highway. Philip remained on his feet, looking baffled and sick. Vish looked out past the road at the ocean, at the gray water barely visible through the thick white layer of fog, and waited for the authorities to find them.

CHAPTER TWENTY-FOUR

IT WAS NIGHT when Officer Guerrero showed up in his hospital room. He'd been there ever since the ambulance had whisked him away that afternoon. A nasty concussion, four broken ribs. No sign of poison in his system, nothing even close, and the kind emergency room doctor had looked at Vish like he was nuts when he'd asked if she could pump his stomach just to be sure. He felt okay now. He felt pretty good, actually, because he was floating on whatever awesome painkillers they'd pumped into him. He greeted Guerrero with a dreamy smile. "Hey, you."

She looked down at him, her face expressionless. "Oh, you'll be fun," she said. She dragged a chair closer to his bedside and sat. He didn't have a private room; there were three other beds lined up beside his, all occupied, so Guerrero reached behind her head and yanked the vinyl curtain around them to give the illusion of privacy. "I'm half tempted to ask you a bunch of questions right now, just to see what your drugged-out answers would be."

"You're not here to question me?" Vish struggled to sit upright. His ribs protested at that, but it was a dull pain, far away.

"Hang on." Guerrero reached over him and fiddled with the controls on the adjustable bed until he was raised to a comfortable sitting position. She smelled like apples and shoe polish. She was in her warm-weather uniform again, her heavy black shoes incongruous with her shorts and short-sleeved top.

She sat on the edge of her chair, both feet planted on the floor, and leaned in to talk to him. She propped her tanned forearms on her thighs. "They've identified eight of the dead kids in that cave, got maybe a dozen more identifications to go. That's not counting the three freshly-charred corpses we found."

"The guys who attacked me. The surfers," Vish said. "I'm not sure how they caught on fire." He was babbling a little, and even in his narcotic haze he knew that was dangerous. There were lies he needed to tell, and Guerrero was sharp enough to see through them if he didn't take some care.

Guerrero held up a hand. "I haven't asked any questions. Stop volunteering answers." She shook her head. "Word from the top brass filtered down to me: You're out of this. You're an innocent bystander who got targeted for no reason, and we're supposed to leave you alone while we sort this mess out."

Vish turned his neck to look at her. The room floated a bit at the movement, which was pleasant. "Really?"

"You got friends in high places, Vish." Guerrero sat up straighter. "So I'm not even supposed to be here, much less ask you questions, which seems all kinds of wrong to me."

"Asking me questions wouldn't help, anyway," Vish said. "I know you don't believe me, but I don't know anything useful."

Officer Guerrero stared at him, then exhaled. "Yeah. So I hear." She got to her feet. "I guess I'll just see you around, Vish." There was a note of warning in her voice that penetrated even through the warm, soupy haze in his head.

"How'd they kill all those people without anyone noticing?" he asked.

"Nobody knew they were missing, for the most part." She shook her head. "We had missing-persons reports on file for some, but they were actors mostly, or singers. A few screenwriters. All of them were living pretty marginal lives. No concerned family members, no one to raise a stink. Most cases, we had no reason to think they hadn't packed up and left town." She twisted her mouth in an ironic smile. "They slipped through the cracks."

Vish hoped he wouldn't see Sparky Mother again. He couldn't get that lucky.

Sparky bore a peace offering in the form of a gigantic flower arrangement, white camellias and flowering jasmine branches and stems of fragrant verbena stuck in a massive silver urn and tied with a blue satin bow. Sparky hovered by his bedside and waggled the arrangement back and forth.

"Poppy's idea," he said. "She chose them. It's generally acknowledged her taste is better than mine."

He plunked the arrangement down on Vish's bedside stand, jostling aside the baby blue teddy bear Mariposa had given to him. It wore a pink t-shirt with a glittery heart on it and clutched a giant heart-shaped lollipop.

Sparky poked the bear with one finger, then glanced at the attached card. "Your fan club?" he asked.

"Is that… thing… dead?" Vish asked. "The thing that had taken over Troy?"

"Nope. Can't happen. But he's learned a lesson about not getting too big for his britches, maybe. Might be a while before he decides to mess with me again."

"Is he going to come after me?" Vish asked.

Sparky cocked his head to one side and mulled this over. "There's no reason for him to, but that doesn't mean he won't. Doesn't matter. I'll look after you."

"That's worked out really well for me thus far."

Sparky snorted. "Okay, sure, I guess I can see where I might not be your favorite person right now. Don't get snotty about it, though. I sort of saved your life."

"You poisoned me," Vish said.

"Nope. I just made you think you were poisoned for a bit. You're fine. I mean, don't get me wrong, I'm sorry about all this." Sparky made a gesture to indicate the hospital bed. "But you're going to be good as new. Better than that, I owe you a serious favor."

Vish glanced at him. Sparky smiled. "I were you, I'd take this opportunity to cash in. We'll get your book published. Or we'll get you a job writing for another television show, one that doesn't suck donkey balls this time."

"I don't want to have anything to do with you," Vish said.

"You sure about that?"

"That I never want to see you again? Absolutely," Vish said. "Anyone ever tell you you're an asshole?"

"Watch it," Sparky said. "I'm feeling kind of warm and fuzzy toward you right now, but even so, it's not a good idea to insult me."

Vish stared at the wall just past the foot of his bed. A television was on somewhere, turned to a news report about the bodies in his cave, but it was out of his line of sight, and anyway, he didn't want to hear anything more about that, not for a long, long time. He didn't trust himself to say anything further to Sparky right now, and he couldn't stand to have him in his room any longer, so he just kept staring at the wall.

Eventually, Sparky sighed. "See you around, Vish," he said, and left.

ACKNOWLEDGMENTS

Special thanks go to Dan Liebke, Ernie Cline and Veronica Viscardi for making gentle and encouraging comments about *Wrong City* when it was in pretty ragged shape, to Morgan Dodge for banging out a fantastic cover in less time than it took to ask if he'd be willing to do it, and to my wonderful aunt Elsbeth Monnett for wanting to read more about Sparky Mother.

ABOUT THE AUTHOR

Born and raised in Spokane, Washington, Morgan Richter graduated with a BFA in Filmic Writing from the University of Southern California's film school. She has worked in production on several TV shows, including *Talk Soup* and *America's Funniest Home Videos*, and has contributed pop culture reviews and essays to websites such as TVgasm and Forces of Geek, as well as to her own site, Preppies of the Apocalypse. She is the owner of Luft Books, an independent publishing company, and the author of *Bias Cut*, *Charlotte Dent*, and *Wrong City*. *Bias Cut* won a silver medal at the 2013 Independent Publishers Book Awards and was a 2012 semi-finalist for the Amazon Breakthrough Novel Award (ABNA). *Charlotte Dent* was a 2008 ABNA semi-finalist. She currently lives in New York City.